becoming clara belle

A NOVEL APPROACH

Libby Layne

Promo

becoming clara belle
by
Libby Layne

© 2010

ISBN: 978-0-9842516-6-7

Cover designed by Amy Jarrett

Warwick House Publishers
720 Court Street
Lynchburg, VA 24504

"Life is a journey and, whether we admit it or not, whether we like it or not, it is, in fact, a journey toward God. There are some people (real or imagined) who will stay with us on the journey, and some who will not. Clara Belle is one of those who will never leave us. She will accompany us, or she will haunt us because, whether we admit it or not, whether we like it or not, she is part of each of us, arguably the best part. This book is essential equipment for the journey."

Reverend Suzanne Currie
First Presbyterian Church
Belle Vernon, Pennsylvania

"Anyone who has known or loved a child who is 'different' will delight in this story. Libby Layne, through Clara Belle, shows clearly how challenging it can be to live as one's authentic self, especially when that "self" does not conform to the expectation of his/her community. Clara Belle's community, in this case, is the very conservative Shenandoah Valley in the 1940s, '50s and '60s. Libby Layne's description of Clara Belle's experiences in this setting perfectly captures the feel of that time and place, as well as depicting her challenges and triumphs. The story of this memorable character provides us with a valuable life lesson and is a truly delightful and thought-provoking read."

Mary Strate Bahn, EdD
Licensed Clinical Psychologist

"Clara Belle takes me back to the magic of Anne of Green Gables. The novel is a coming of age story with a heroine full of courage and fun as she deals with the problems and pain of being different. A book that will delight readers from age 12 to 112."

Betsy Garrard
High School English Teacher

"Libby Layne skillfully brings her readers into Clara Belle's life, then takes them along on her journey. They will join her through the stages of her slow development from a child with multiple insecurities to a young adult with budding confidence. Clara Belle's irreverent witticisms are both hilarious and contagious. The strong sense of family in her life, especially her Aunt Belle, is central to why Clara Belle triumphs in the end."

Linda Abbey Buck
Special Education Teacher

To Aunt Libby
the original "gypsy goddess"

"…a story is a letter the author writes to himself, to tell himself things that he would be unable to discover otherwise."

Carlos Ruiz Zafon
Shadow of the Wind

Prologue

"Hey, Doo-Dah, what's invisible and smells like carrots?"

Her stage was the hayloft of their granddaddy Miller's barn, one of the few that had survived Sheridan's burning raids in the Shenandoah Valley during the Civil War. Her strange alto voice was already loud, but the walls and massive beams, built of aging heart pine, carried her loaded question to every nook and cranny of their favorite hideaway on the farm. Pigeons in the rafters scattered in a noisy flurry of feathers and poop, as if they, too, waited for the answer to her riddle. She had chosen the precise area on the loft where an open window behind her, near the top of the barn, focused down a dust-filled sunbeam like a theater spotlight.

Her sunlit hair—strawberry-colored, pink and frizzy, maniacally framed a face much too small for the wide-spaced, oddly shaped eyes. Quarter-inch thick glasses slid down her freckled nose and would have fallen off had there not been a just-in-time upturn. Her mouth, like her eyes, seemed oversized for her face and was stretched wide in an outrageous grin. She had put together an equally outrageous costume. Her signature pair of puffy pantaloons, made from a gaudy print of bright yellow sunflowers on a purple background, were topped by one of Jordan's hand-me-down Superman T-shirts, three sizes too big, and a red-and-white polka-dot vest she had taken from the church Salvation Army box when no one was looking. The finishing touch to her ensemble was a ratty, white stocking cap that she always seemed to put on inside out and backward.

She stood barely as high as the bale of hay next to her and only the fullness of her pants hid the bulge of what Jordan knew to be a leg brace attached to one of her scuffed brown shoes.

1

"I don't know, Clara Belle," Jordan answered, as he always did. "What's invisible and smells like carrots?"

He waited while she paused dramatically, allowing sufficient time to build the suspense of the moment before her grand finale.

"BUNNY FARTS! TA-DAH!"

Both arms shot up in the air in the triumphant gesture of a clown who had pulled off the perfect prank. Knowing what was expected of him, her only audience other than the pigeons, Jordan immediately hooted, clapped and stomped his approval. She executed a deep theatrical bow accepting his adoration as she gushed, "Thank you, thank you very much," then collapsed on the floor in a pile of hay and giggles.

She was four years old.

Foreword

I wrote the previous prologue twelve years ago. In the years since, only *that* passage remains exactly as I wrote it then—only *that* Clara Belle remained unchanged.

I had been invited to give a little talk about Epiphany at a Wednesday night church supper in January of 1998. I have no idea why I was asked to speak on this particular subject. I certainly knew little about the Epiphany event or season, having grown up in a non-liturgical church, and even thirty years as an Episcopalian had not prepared me to speak of what the occasion meant to me personally. I did some digging around for definitions of the word itself and examples of what Epiphany might evoke in one's daily and spiritual life.

I began my speech that night in an appropriate, semi-serious vein, citing my quotes and definitions concerning Epiphany. Within five minutes I had segued skillfully into my comfort zone—humor and silliness.

"Epiphany," I explained, "was when Jesus stood up, raised his hands in the air and announced, 'Ta-Dah, this is who I Am!' "

"We are called to respond, as Captain Hook did to his sidekick, 'Smee, I just had an Apostrophe!' "

I continued in this light-hearted manner to the end of my talk. Everyone laughed, I felt gratified, I executed my final "Ta-Dah" and started home, immediately descending into major guilt mode. Had I been irreverent, sacrilegious, disrespectful? Had I, once again, resorted to being on stage, entertaining the audience? Might I have better chosen to be more religious and devout in telling my faith story?

I struggled with this for several days, beating myself up for being such a show-off, such a clown. I'm not sure when my own personal "Apostrophe" finally manifested, but the result was the birth of Clara Belle Miller.

I decided that the best venue for telling the story of Clara Belle was the novel. I had already self-published my own memoirs several years before, chronicling my adventures with wild dolphins and autistic children. Fiction would lend itself well to this character, part autobiographical, part based on the children with whom I had worked in previous years. I would set the action on the farm where generations of my family had grown up. I would tell stories from my own experience and tales of a diverse and unique family of parents, grandparents, siblings, cousins, aunts and uncles who all lived within ten miles of each other. The book would write itself, "a piece of cake," I casually surmised, owing to the myriad characters and family lore from which I could draw.

I would write the novel on our annual RV trip to Florida in February. My husband and I would be gone a full month which would provide an extended time away from the busyness of home — a concentrated writing period with few distractions, excluding Mickey and Minnie Mouse, of course.

I began writing on a yellow legal pad with a #2 pencil. The Prologue, a description of my first glimpse of Clara Belle, flowed easily and I couldn't write fast enough. This was going to be fun.

In the succeeding years, not one word of Clara Belle's story was published in any form. There were seven printed-out hard copy versions, as well as several other drafts languishing in the files on my computer. There were three years of black folders filled with reads, re-reads, notes and critiques from two professional, and very well paid, editors who encouraged me profusely, taught me abundantly but in the end agreed, "You have no plot." I had packed up the lot of it and lugged the large cardboard box to my attic until…

When I began to assemble and rework Clara Belle's story this time around, I was faced with a formidable task.

There were copious versions that spanned an unwieldy fifty years of her life and were told from multiple points of view. In re-reading the material I discovered that, without exception, I liked the very first version best. In spite of the lack of slick literary form and technique, the heart of the story of Clara Belle beat strong and sure. I also discovered that with each succeeding attempt to find a plot, I had squeezed the very life out of that heart.

In this final version, you'll find a collection of good stories about Clara Belle and the Miller family. Often, the point of view changes and there may be characters you haven't met who tell a particular Clara Belle tale simply because I happened to like that perspective. There may be sections that veer off the story line; there may be things left hanging or leaps of age and time passing. My former editors insisted that I never developed a strong plot line. If that is true, the order in which the stories are told or who tells them doesn't matter. I believe that what does matter is Clara Belle's journey. That's plot enough for me.

There are seasons when the tree is green, there are seasons when it is dry, and seasons when for the life of us, the thing looks dead. Now does this mean you are serving some capricious God who comes and goes by whim? Or, could it be, that it is only through SEASONS that true growth may come?

Gene Edwards
An Inward Journey

BOOK I

THE SEASON OF BECLOWNING

Chapter 1

THE CLOWN FOR CHRISTMAS
December 1940

"Her does too look like a clown."

"Shush, Jordan, not so loud; it's just that little suit she has on."

But even he could see that the red and white polka dot pajamas with yellow cotton balls marching down the front were just the beginning.

She was the puniest thing he'd ever seen—except a new-hatched peepy, maybe. Her hands and feet were swallowed up by the clown pajamas they'd given her when Aunt Mary Faith and Uncle Ben Jr. finally brought her home from the hospital. Jordan had gone with his mother to the Cradle Shop, the only store in Harrisonburg that carried baby clothes, and they'd bought the littlest size.

Her lopsided head was covered with a pinkish-red, cotton candy-looking frizz. Her skin was yellowish and the red spots on her cheeks and nose made her look even more like a clown. He could see that her nose and ears weren't finished yet and her eyes were weird-shaped. They reminded him of the nuts on top of an Almond Joy candy bar, but were blue, not brown.

Jordan felt his own eyes with his fingers—they were right beside his nose on each side. Clara Belle's eyes were real close to her ears and the outside corners were tilted up catawampus.

Clara Belle's white wicker-basket sat in the middle of Granddaddy Miller's bed, almost buried in the big pile of the Miller clan's winter wraps. Jordan leaned over the edge of the basket to get a closer look at the strange baby inside.

"You a baby clown?"

She looked at him with those slanty eyes and Jordan could have sworn she nodded her head.

"Jordan, I have to go help with breakfast; why don't you go play with the other kids?" his mother said.

"I wanna stay here and play with Clara Belle."

"She's way too little to play with yet."

"Her tole me she was lonesome in here."

His mother smiled.

"Well, all right, but just look, don't touch her or anything."

As soon as his mother left the room, Jordan went back to his talk with Clara Belle.

"Hi, Clara Belle. I'm Jordan, and I'm four years older dan you. I can run real fast and Santa Claus bringed me a new red truck for Christmas. But you can't play with it yet because you're too little. I can count to twenty—one, two three, four, five, eleven, sixteen, twenty—and I can turn a summersault. Watch."

He jumped off the bed, squatted down, lowered his head and rolled over sideways, bumping into Grandmother Miller's dressing table.

"Ow!" he muttered, not wanting her to know it hurt.

He picked himself up and got back up on the bed.

"Whatcha think 'bout dat?"

The strange baby stared at him and didn't seem to think it was all that great.

"Jordan, come on now and eat breakfast," he heard his mother call from the doorway.

He wasn't quite ready to end his visit with his new clown-cousin, but he followed his mother out into the crowd of Millers piling in for this year's Christmas breakfast. Aunt Belle had just come through the front door with Uncle Henry who was carrying her laundry basket full of presents. Jordan tried to figure out which one of the packages might be his— he loved the way they were wrapped. Everyone knew that when Aunt Belle ran out of Christmas paper, she used the funny papers and when she ran out of those, she just left whatever she'd bought in the Sears or J.C. Penney's paper bag. No one ever cared—hers were always the best presents.

Uncle Henry set the basket beside the tree and then disappeared out back with several of the other uncles. (Everyone knew what they were doing.) Aunt Belle went straight to the kitchen to help the other aunts get breakfast ready.

Jordan's mother led him back to the long, skinny back porch where the children's table was set up.

"Sit down, Jordan. I'll go get your plate."

"Nobody's here yet. Can't I go play with Clara Belle till Susan and Hank Jr. eat?"

"You stay put. I'll go get them. Clara Belle's probably asleep by now anyhow."

As his mother left, Jordan heard a loud whoop from the living room, which meant another Miller family had come through the front door. Then, like somebody had turned the knob of the radio, the noise cranked up another notch. By the time all the Millers arrived, you had to shout if you wanted anybody to hear you. Millers liked to celebrate—a lot and loud.

The grownups ate in shifts around the big oak table in the dining room. For Christmas morning, Grandmother Miller had put in all four leaves.

Next to the dining room, in the tiny kitchen, the aunts cooked mountains of food on an old gas stove. Jordan forgot all about Clara Belle when he smelled the bacon and sausage cooking in the big iron skillets.

"Can I help, Aunt Belle?" he asked as he watched her take a large fork and lift out the crispy strips of bacon, four at a time, then put them on a paper napkin.

"Uh-uh, Jordan, hot grease might getcha. But when I get to the eggs, you can help me stir."

She pulled a chair up to the stove and pointed, "Up here."

He crawled up on the chair by Aunt Belle. He saw Aunt Lillian frown—he didn't care—she was always grouchy.

"Move back while I…" She poured all but a little of the hot bacon grease into an empty tin can, then dumped a huge bowl of yellow, beaten eggs into the hot skillet. She stirred the eggs around and around with a wooden spoon. When she scraped the bottom of the skillet and lifted the cooked pieces to the top, the runny eggs ran in to take their place and made a yummy, sizzling sound.

"Now you." He put his hand over Aunt Belle's and helped her stir—Jordan liked the feel and sound of the scraping and sizzling. Aunt Belle knew just how long to cook the eggs so that they were fluffy, not dry, which was exactly the way he liked them.

Jordan watched Aunt Lillian line up slices of soft, white bread, one side buttered, on a cookie sheet and shove them into the oven. He knew that when they came out, the bottoms would be crunchy and the tops would be soft and bubbly; that was exactly the way he liked them.

When the toast went in, Aunt Bootie took out the Pyrex bowl of "scalped" oysters he and his mother had put together at home last night. They smelled like something really good, but Jordan had seen the snotty stuff those things were fished out of so he wanted no part of them. The grown-ups always drooled over the oysters so he supposed that nobody but he and his mother knew what they looked like beforehand, and they weren't telling.

"OK shite-poke, skedaddle, thanks for the hand." Aunt Belle lifted him down and headed him toward the porch door. His older cousins were already there.

"Don't take any scalloped oysters," whispered Susan to her brother Hank Jr. as they sat at the children's table. "You know the rule. You gotta clean your plate or no dessert."

"I bet wittle Jordan has to eat'em cause his mommy made'em," said Hank Jr. in a mean voice.

"Don't neither. I can *not* eat anything I want."

When his mother came around with the oysters he shook his head, no, but she gave him a spoonful anyway.

Hank Jr. smiled.

"I saw you talking to Aunt Mary Faith's baby in the bedroom like she was normal or something," he said. "Didn't you know she's a retard?"

"You better stop saying stuff like that," said Susan. "You know how Mom is about Clara Belle."

"Well, she is. I heard she was born way too early and she'll never be right in the head."

Jordan scraped the oysters off the side of his plate into his paper napkin.

"Was not talking to'er."

"Were too, I heard you. You better stay away from her—might be catchy."

"Leave Jordan alone, Hank Jr.," said Susan. "He's only four. Don't pay any attention to him, Jordan. You can like Clara Belle if you want to."

"I don't," he said, ducking his head and finishing his scrambled eggs. "OK, I'm done. I want some dessert."

On the card table next to them, spread with a red tablecloth, were plates filled with cake, gooey cinnamon "sticky buns" and Christmas sugar cookies decorated with sprinkles of red and green sugar. Christmas was the one and only time when dessert was allowed at breakfast.

"I'm done, too," said Hank Jr., reaching for the very cookie Jordan had planned to pick. "Now let's get out to the steps and wait for presents."

Jordan took his second choice cookie and sat down to eat it while his older cousins left him alone on the porch.

Jordan's aunts were busy clearing tables and washing dishes, and, as he wandered through the dining room looking for his mother, he overheard them, all talking at once. Jordan stayed outside the kitchen door when he heard Clara Belle's name.

"Sure don't think that little Clara Belle looks right."

12

"Specially 'round the eyes."

"Mongoloid-lookin' if you ask me."

"Doesn't cry a bit, even with all this noise. You know—"

"Tiniest thing I ever saw. No bigger'n a minute," said his mother.

"Mary Faith and Ben Jr. haven't said much, but betcher boots they're worried."

"For sure there are places for such as her. It wonders me the doctors let a bubbelly like her come home yet," said old Aunt Lillian who, besides being a grouch, talked funny.

Aunt Mary Faith walked up behind Jordan and everything went quiet. Aunt Belle had been drying dishes, not saying a word. When she turned and saw the two of them, she threw her dish towel straight at Aunt Lillian and pushed through the aunts. Taking his hand, she said, "Hey kiddo, lets us go see that beautiful baby girl," and without looking back, the three of them marched out of the room.

They went back into Granddaddy Miller's bedroom, where the mountain of coats now made a fort around Clara Belle's basket. Jordan climbed the wall of wraps and looked at the baby everyone in the kitchen had been talking about.

"Hey, big boy, wanna—" She rocked her arms like a cradle.

"Oh, I don't think so, Belle," Aunt Mary Faith said. "She's so fragile and Jordan doesn't know how to hold a baby."

"Don't need a thing but that pillow over there. Jordan!"

Jordan threw the pillow from Granddaddy Miller's bed to Aunt Belle.

"Well, all right, I guess we can do that, but be very careful, Jordan."

"Yes, Ma'am, I promise," he said.

"Sit," Aunt Belle said, motioning him to get up on Grandmother Miller's bed. He crawled up and leaned back against the headboard. Aunt Belle fluffed the pillow and laid it on his lap, then took two more from Granddaddy Miller's bed and placed them on either side.

"Perfect."

Aunt Mary Faith carefully picked up Clara Belle like she was holding a new baby kitten. Even when she held up Clara Belle's skinny neck, the baby's head wobbled precariously.

"Is her head stuck on tight enough?" Jordan asked, imagining it falling off and rolling across the floor. Aunt Mary Faith gave him a look.

Aunt Belle just smiled and took Clara Belle from Aunt Mary Faith. She whispered something in Clara Belle's ear.

"Did you tell her a secret?" Jordan asked.

"A very important one," said Aunt Belle as she laid the baby on the pillow in Jordan's lap.

"Tell me, too."

"Maybe some day—when you need it."

He held his breath, then let it out and looked down at his tiny cousin. Her Almond Joy eyes met his and he had the strangest feeling that even though this was the first time he'd ever seen her, they'd known each other for a really long time. And what was even stranger, he believed she knew this, too.

"That's enough," said Aunt Mary Faith, scooping up Clara Belle. Jordan was not ready to give her up just yet and he stared at the little dent she had made in the pillow. He touched it with his hand—it was still warm. He leaned over and pressed his nose to the place she had lain—it smelled like baby powder and sour milk where she had spit up.

Just then he saw Hank Jr. at the door watching—he was grinning a sneaky grin.

Chapter 2

THE CHOOSING

"Hey, anybody want presents?" yelled Uncle Jim.

"Yeah, me," Jordan cried, leaping from his nest of pillows. Jordan ran past Hank Jr. to his place on the staircase in the front hall where they would wait for the presents to be handed out from the living room. The older cousins sat at the top of the twenty-step staircase and the younger ones sat at the bottom. Jordan's place was on the fifth step.

Jordan peeked around the corner where Granddaddy and Grandmother Miller were sitting—they looked like a king and queen on their thrones in their big wing chairs in front of a plastered-over fireplace. There were fireplaces in every room of the old house, even the bedrooms, and every one of them had been put out of commission with bricks and plaster at one time or another.

"Hey, Susan," Jordan said, "you think Granddaddy's tryin' to keep somethin' in or somethin' out?"

"What the heck are you talkin' about, Bozo-Baby-lover," said Hank Jr.

"The fireplaces, I mean… and don't call me that."

He looked at Susan.

"They just don't use them anymore, Jordan, because they're too old and full of soot. Hank Jr., you better stop it or I'm gonna tell."

"I bet Santa just flies right over. Too many old people here anyways," Jordan said.

"You don't believe—"

"Hank Jr., enough," Aunt Belle's head popped around the door.

In the corner of the room stood the little cedar tree that Jordan and his father had chopped down in the back field the week before, now decorated with colored lights, glass ornaments and shiny, silver icicles. There were so many presents crammed under the tree that they almost reached over to where Granddaddy and Grandmother Miller sat—there was hardly a place to walk.

"Here, Jordan," said Aunt Belle. She always went into the pile looking for one with his name so he wouldn't have to wait too long.

She handed the box to the cousins on the first two steps and they passed it up to Jordan. He could see right off by the shape of the box that inside were either socks or mittens. He ripped off the paper, hoping he was wrong; he wasn't. There were two pairs of socks—one green, one red. The color of the socks wasn't that bad, but they were those awful thin and stretchy kind like the preacher, Reverend Showalter, wore. He set the box down and waited for another present.

"Jordan, don't forget to save the tag," his mother said as she picked up the box. "You need to thank whoever gave these to you."

"But they're ugly. Why do I have to pretend I like'um. I'm not ever gonna wear—"

"Not so loud, Jordan."

"Hank Jr., this one's for you," said Aunt Belle.

"Susan, here ya go."

"This says 'to Kate and Joe.' " Jordan's mother took the large box and gave it to his dad to open.

"Barbara Ann, here's one from Granddaddy and Grandmother Miller."

More and more presents were given out and the pile was getting smaller and smaller.

Jordan was getting worried. He still hadn't gotten his present from Aunt Belle and Uncle Henry. He could always depend on them to pick out something wonderful. Some years they came up with a toy he hadn't even imagined.

They always seemed to know when there was some hot new thing in the store and were also the first ones to get it.

The next present he opened was a set of three Golden Books: *The Three Little Pigs, Little Red Riding Hood, and The Three Billy Goats Gruff.* Pretty good, but still not the one he was waiting for.

As soon as he opened the box, he knew who had given him the gift. Inside were two plastic bags full of fish food and a little net with a long handle. Aunt Bootie always gave Jordan something weird. Every year his mother would say, "It's the thought that counts," and every year Jordan wondered what in the world Aunt Bootie must be thinking. She had succeeded at weirdness again. Jordan didn't have any fish.

A pair of mittens was next, then two toy trucks, a bag of hard candy, a new set of jack rocks, a big rubber ball and a jump rope.

"Here's yours from Granddaddy and Grandmother Miller," his mother said, handing him a really big box—he knew it was clothes. Grandmother Miller was too old and there were too many grandchildren for her to shop for, so she gave money to the mothers who always bought clothes. Jordan wished his mother would get him toys, but she never did. This year she'd picked out a fire-engine red jacket with a hood and a front zipper which, for being something to wear, wasn't half bad.

"Jordan, got your name on it," said Aunt Belle, handing him a medium-size package wrapped in Dagwood and Blondie. Finally.

"Thank you, Aunt Belle," he said because, even before he opened it, he knew it would be just what he wanted. He ripped open the paper as fast as he could and threw it into the pile on the floor. On the box was a picture of a train that looked just like *The Little Engine That Could*, Jordan's favorite book. Before he could open the box his mother whisked it away.

"Jordan, let's wait till we get home to take it out. We don't want to lose any of the parts."

"But, Mommy—"

"Don't argue."

"Can we go home now?"

"Not yet. We've still got the envelopes."

When all the presents were handed out and opened, the paper on the living room floor was piled high as Jordan's head. He was the first one to jump into the ocean of Christmas wrapping, making waves with his play-swimming. Soon all the cousins were thrashing around and making a racket.

"Stop, you nit-wit kids, no more swimming in this living room, yet," Granddaddy Miller yelled, as he was walloped in the leg with Hank Jr.'s backstroke. He talked funny, too, but that was OK because, well, because he was Granddaddy.

The time had come for the grown-ups' favorite part of Christmas morning: Granddaddy Miller was about to give out the white envelopes that were propped on the limbs of the Christmas tree. Aunt Pearl plucked them off like golden apples, handed them to Granddaddy, and he called out the names one at a time. Each of the grandchildren got an envelope, too, but their parents snatched them away quickly so they wouldn't be dropped in the Christmas wrapping ocean and go out with the tide of trash. Inside the envelopes were crisp green bills; not even the grown-ups knew from year to year how much they'd get. This year Jordan's had a five on it. He didn't know what the grown-ups got but the number was most likely more than five. He noticed that when they thanked Granddaddy, they weren't pretending. Jordan's parents had started letting him keep a little of the money to spend on anything he wanted at Glen's Fairprice Store. The rest they took away and put in the bank, which just meant he couldn't spend it.

As the grown-ups sifted through the wrapping paper for lost presents, Jordan took a quick look around for Hank Jr., and then wandered back into the bedroom to take another peek at Clara Belle. He climbed up on the bed. She was lying so still that if her eyes hadn't been open, he would have sworn she was asleep. He leaned over the basket.

"Lookie what I got, Clara Belle," he said, holding his big red ball over the side of the basket. Aunt Mary Faith walked up behind him and said, "What are you doing, Jordan?" He was so surprised that he almost dropped the ball on top of Clara Belle. His aunt yanked him off the bed by the arm and Jordan started to cry. His mother heard the commotion and, as she rushed into the room, she said, "Get your coat and hat, Jordan. It's time to go home. Sorry, Mary Faith."

"I can't find 'um," he whimpered, without even looking. Since Jordan and his family lived closest to Granddaddy's and were the first ones to get there, their wraps were always at the bottom of the pile. His mother dug and dug and found his hat and coat with his mittens still tucked in the pockets.

"Can I tell Clara Belle bye, Aunt Mary Faith? Please?"

"May I, Jordan, may I," she said.

"*May* I say goodbye, please?"

"Yes you may, but you must be very careful."

Jordan looked into the basket one last time and saw that Clara Belle's strange eyes were closed.

He whispered, "Bye, Clara Belle, see ya sometime."

"Not so loud, Jordan," his mother said, like always.

He put on his hat, coat and mittens and walked with his father out to the car. He got into the back seat and while he waited for his parents to finish saying goodbye to everyone, Aunt Belle came to the window.

"Clara Belle's a special gift," she said in a mysterious voice. "You already know that part, right, Jordan?"

"I guess so," Jordan said, not sure he really did.

"Never forget you two'll be special cousins to each other growin' up," she said. "You'll teach her some important things and she'll teach you some important things." She pointed to her heart. "Listen right here when it comes to Clara Belle, not other people. You're lucky she chose you."

He watched as Uncle Ben Jr. and Aunt Mary Faith put Clara Belle's basket in their Dodge station wagon. They looked sad.

As they drove back down the lane, Jordan asked himself: What did Aunt Belle mean when she said Clara Belle had chosen him? What did she choose him for? Did it have anything to do with what Hank Jr. and Susan were talking about? He didn't understand, but he knew that if Aunt Belle had said such a thing, it was, for sure, true. But on a Christmas Day, questions aren't nearly as important as other things; he hadn't even played with the Santa Claus toys under his own tree yet.

Chapter 3

THE DOO-DAH DAY

Mary Faith looked out her living room window. The summer sun made the corn silks on the tall stalks across the lane shine like—well, like silk. She smiled—who would have thought a city girl like her would have loved living here?

Miller's Barn Farm stretched 350 acres in all directions from Granddaddy Miller's in an area known, to a select few, as "Lick-Skillet." The lane turned off Route 42 and wound its way back over the hill to reach the old house and barn. If you met someone coming the other way, you had to drive completely off the road; if the other vehicle was a farm truck, you just prayed.

Jordan's parents, Kate and Joe Glick, had built "the little house" on the sharp curve about halfway up the lane as their first home. Kate Miller was the second eldest of Ben Jr.'s five sisters. Jordan was born nine months later, and when Emily was born three years after that, they built a larger house around the corner and left the little house empty.

After three miscarriages, Mary Faith finally became pregnant with Clara Belle. Her doctors advised her to quit work. Money got tight, so she and Ben Jr. moved from Harrisonburg to the farm and into the little house. He was not happy about leaving the city house—he considered the move a step down in the world.

She walked to the place in the hall where she could see every room in the tiny house. Behind her was the bath and bedroom, to her right was the kitchen and dining room, and straight ahead was the living room where Clara Belle's wooden crib sat in front of the small fireplace. Out the front door was a stoop with two white columns holding up a shingled overhang. The effect was distinctly doll-house-like and she felt a bit like a little girl playing mother and father and baby.

Her real doll was now two years old, sitting on the floor playing with her toys.

"Hello, little one. How's my big girl? Now what are we going to do today?"

"Exactly what she does every other day," said Ben Jr., coming out of the bedroom, tucking in his shirt.

"What time's your first class?"

"It's not going to make any difference how much time you spend with her, you know, she'll never be able to do anything. All my sisters say the same thing—except Belle, of course, but everyone knows she comes from an entirely different planet. I don't think it's a good idea letting her spend so much time at Belle's either. You know how—"

"Coming home for supper?"

"Why? You know what you'll be doing."

"She takes a lot of time, Ben."

He muttered something, put his books and papers in his briefcase and started out the door.

"She's a gift, you know."

"Don't start with the God talk."

Mary Faith suddenly realized that there was someone lurking outside the door.

"We'll talk about this some other time," she said, nodding her head toward the porch. "Come on in, Jordan. Clara Belle's waiting for you."

Ben Jr. stomped out the door onto the little front porch where Jordan stood cowering. Without acknowledging the boy's presence, he marched to his car and left for work.

"Maybe from now on you should wait until you see your Uncle Ben has gone to work before you come over."

Mary Faith glanced from Jordan down to Clara Belle who sat on a blanket on the floor, taking it all in.

"Sorry, little one, Daddy's just...tired. Glad you came over, Jordan. What do you want to do today?"

"What we always do, I guess. She learned to walk yet?"

"Give her time; she's just getting the hang of crawling. Watch this."

Mary Faith turned Clara Belle on her stomach and she quickly dug her right elbow and heel into the carpet and scooted across the floor like a bug. She looked up at Jordan and smiled. Her smile started as a twinkle in her blue eyes, then moved down to wrinkle up her pug nose; that made her eyes scrunch shut. Finally, her smile arrived at her lips, where it turned up the corners in a closed-mouth grin.

"She smiles like the monkey on the M page of my ABC book," he said.

Mary Faith felt the familiar glitch in her stomach.

"She's not easy to get to smile and I think she smiles at you more than anybody."

"I know why that is," said Jordan. "Aunt Belle told me Christmas."

"Well, whatever the reason, you sure are special to her and you're a big help to me. You notice anything different about Clara Belle's eyes?"

Taped to her face was a tiny pair of glasses.

Jordan moved closer and looked again.

"Why'd she have to get those? Her eyes look fine to me."

"They are a beautiful blue, aren't they?"

Jordan waited.

Mary Faith knew he wouldn't be satisfied until she explained.

"Clara Belle was born way too early and was so little they gave her oxygen at the hospital to breathe better."

"But why did that make her not be able to see right?" Jordan asked.

"The doctors didn't mean to, but they gave her too much."

She saw the wheels turning in his head.

"But if oxygen is a good thing and we gotta have it to breathe, how come you can get too much?"

"I don't know, Jordan, sometimes it—"

"Hey, what if I ran too fast and started breathing gobs and gobs of oxygen, and then I got too much, could my eyes get fuzzy like Clara Belle's?"

"I don't—"

"Betcha that's what old Aunt Lillian was talking about when she told me to stop running around—said it was too much of a good thing. I gotta be more careful."

Mary Faith laughed. "Don't think I'd worry too much about Aunt Lillian. She gets a little cranky sometimes and says things. Keep up the running."

"Those glasses make her kinda look like a frog."

Mary Faith winced again. She still hadn't gotten used to any comment about Clara Belle's looks, even Jordan's innocent frankness. She accepted all of her daughter's limitations without judgment; however, she was sensitive to others' perceptions. They only underscored Ben Jr.'s constant reminders of Clara Belle's differences.

"Why don't you tell Clara Belle the story of *The Little Engine That Could*? That's her favorite one."

"How'd you know—she tell you that?"

"Now, Jordan, you know she doesn't talk. But I can just tell. All you have to do is look at her face. She talks without words—she smiles, she frowns, she cries, and sometimes you can even tell by the way she moves. I know what she wants just by paying attention and I bet you can, too."

"I guess."

"I'm going to put a load of wash in. Could you watch her for a minute?"

"Sure, I've got something important to tell her anyways. Can we go out on the porch?"

"Let me put her in her swing; she might crawl off."

Mary Faith picked up Clara Belle and carried her to the baby swing on the front porch.

"Watch this." As Clara Belle was placed in the swing, she began smiling and moving all over. "You see, she's telling us that she likes being outside in her swing with you and that she's ready to hear what you have to say."

"She told you all that?"

"Sure did. You just have to understand her language, that's all."

"I'll try."

Mary Faith went back into the house but lingered just inside the screen door.

"Clara Belle," Jordan said as he sat down in front of the swing, "I'm gonna tell you somethin' real important and, when I tell you, I wan'cha to answer in your language and I'll try to understand like your mom. Here goes. I start school soon and can't come over much anymore."

He sat, waiting for a reaction.

"Didja hear me? I won't be able to read to you or teach you songs until after school. That means you have to get along all day without me."

Again, he waited. No response.

He stood up, "I don't care what your mom says, you don't have a language."

Suddenly her blue eyes widened behind her frog-glasses and she spoke.

"D-Doo-Dah, D-Doo-Dah."

Jordan's mouth dropped open. Mary Faith held her breath behind the screen door.

She said it again, "Doo-Dah, D-Doo-Dah" and Jordan yelled, "You're saying my name, you're saying my name! Jordan—Doo-Dah—Jordan—Doo-Dah. You can talk. Aunt Mary Faith, come here quick! Clara Belle is saying my name. You were right—she does have a language."

Mary Faith was already on the porch.

"You're talking, you can… I just knew it," she said, plucking Clara Belle from the swing. The baby was as surprised as anyone at the sound she made and kept saying her new word over and over. It was then that Mary Faith noticed something a bit odd. Instead of a sweet little girl voice, Clara Belle's was very low and loud, almost a croak. She looked at Jordan.

He shrugged, "Who cares?"

Chapter 4

THE LEARNING CURVE

"You ready to go meet the bus, Jordan?" his mother asked.

"Been ready for an hour," said his father. "Never did see a kid so darn excited 'bout goin' to school in my life. I sure wasn't."

"You went to Broadway High," said his mother. "You never heard all the tales of the great Dayton High like he has all these years. That place was the best thing that ever happened to us Millers—got us off the farm to the big city of Dayton."

From the end of the lane to the town of Dayton was about two miles south down Route 42. Dayton was a country town of barely five hundred, a figure that included pets. The tiny metropolis was chock-full of schools of lower and higher learning, three churches that preached mainstream religion, (nothing occult like Catholic), and the citizens considered it a hub for cultural activities, such as the annual Garden Club Flower Show and piano recitals at the Conservatory. There was even talk of a little scandal or two—something about Fred Ellison, the president of the bank, running off with a lady teller who had helped him embezzle some money. Main Street offered to the fine people of Dayton, as well as the county folk who came in from the sticks, Virgil's Texaco station, J.B. Skinner's Grocery and Waller's General Store, The First National Bank, a United States Post Office, Carl's Barber Shop, Shenandoah Printers, Lottie's Bakery, a soda shop teenage hangout called The Pantry, Welby Skinner's poultry dressing plant and, at the far end, Martin's Farm Machinery. Along this same stretch of less than a mile stood the Brethren and United Brethren churches, as well as family homes and a few small apartments. If you took a sharp right at the bank building about halfway down Main, and doubled back on College Street, you could find Betsy's Beauty Shop, Shenandoah Printers and, farther down, the Shenandoah Conservatory of Music. Off to the left of College Street and up the hill was Dayton High School.

The building sat on top of the hill like a large brick fortress with the white pillars of a southern mansion. To reach the entrance from the street you had to climb three sets of cement steps, which were bordered on both sides by a terraced green lawn. Through this entrance had walked Jordan's mother, every one of his aunts and most of his uncles. In rooms with fourteen-foot ceilings and rows of pine desks linked together with wrought-iron frames, they had remained for an education that spanned grades one through twelve. The advantages of this way of educating children were many. Elementary school children were exposed on a daily basis to upperclassmen who modeled leadership qualities they could observe and imitate. Each grade level had its rites of passage, which were well established and understood by each student. There was a natural progression from elementary to high school with no adjustment to moving to a completely different building. Most teachers had taught the same grades for years so they were familiar to everyone. The entire system provided an atmosphere of continuity and security. Jordan had a sense, even in the first grade, that he was part of something important and at this school would grow up to take his place in the scheme of things there.

"Is it time to go yet?" asked Jordan. "I'm tired of waiting."

"You want to ride down with me in the back of the pickup? I'm going into town to get some feed."

"Uh-uh, Mom, I wanna walk, but couldja pick me up after school when the bus lets me off? I need to get right over to Clara Belle's soon as I get home to tell her everything."

"Can't do that, Jordan; I'll be right in the middle of vaccinating new calves. You'll just have to walk up, get your snack and go on over then. How about staying here and playing with Emily awhile?"

"Emily's no fun, and anyways, Clara Belle needs me. Hey, I'd better go over and tell her goodbye."

"Have a good day, son," said his father.

"Better hurry," said his mother. "Don't want to miss the bus the first day. Goodbye, Jordan."

"Bye," said Jordan, running out the back door and across the lawn to the little house.

He ran up the steps of the porch and knocked on the door. Mary Faith peeked out the window. When she saw who it was, she disappeared for a moment and then reappeared with Clara Belle in her arms.

"I came to tell her goodbye, but I gotta do it quick, so's I won't miss the bus, so bye, Clara Belle. See you right after school."

As he turned to leave, Clara Belle ceremoniously raised her right arm in the air and in her low, croaky voice said, "D-Doo-Dah, D-Doo-Dah."

Jordan felt like he'd been blessed by the preacher.

~

Jordan's great interest in Clara Belle was barely noticed by his parents until he had started school. Relationships between the Miller cousins were traditionally close. The Miller aunts served as babysitters for Jordan when his parents went out for a special occasion and the Miller cousins were his best friends. They often spent the night at one another's houses.

During the next two years, Jordan's parents expected him to lose interest in Clara Belle. He had always been rather shy and quiet with few friends except his cousins.

29

"Jordan, why don't you have one of your classmates over after school sometime?" asked his mother.

"Nobody could come anyways," he said. "Most all live on farms and have chores."

After school, Jordan did his homework with Clara Belle, reading *Dick and Jane* books and working arithmetic. He taught her songs and games he had learned at school and the more he learned, the more she learned. He was doing exactly what Aunt Belle had predicted; he was Clara Belle's teacher and loved every minute of his duties as her tutor. Aunt Mary Faith, forever the school teacher, also worked with Clara Belle, assuming, as did everyone else, that she would never go to public school. Aunt Mary Faith bravely ignored the pressures of both family and society and dedicated herself to rearing Clara Belle as any other child.

Another of Jordan's self-appointed duties as Clara Belle's "chosen" was to defend her to anyone who doubted her potential.

"Clara Belle's so, so smart, Mom, you'd never believe it," said Jordan. "She reads as good as I can and knows all the words to songs I teach her. Why can't she go to school when she's old enough? She'd do good as anybody."

"Jordan, Clara Belle's just different, that's all. Schools aren't set up for re...for children like her and she'd be out of place and probably not be treated well by the other kids. From what you say, poor little Clara Belle can do a lot more than we ever thought, but she still can't walk without her brace, she's got those thick glasses, she stutters and, well, she's just plain different."

"Everybody's wrong about Clara Belle. And don't call her 'poor little Clara Belle.' She's not poor little anything and she's not retarded either. OK, she looks different, but that's just because she was born way too soon. It doesn't make her dumb. She's real, real smart. She knows more big words than I do. You wait and see. We'll show all of you. Especially mean old Aunt Lillian."

Chapter 5

THE PARLOR AT AUNT BELLE'S

Every Saturday, without fail, Aunt Belle drove from her house in Hinton to Miller's Barn Farm and picked up her niece for the morning until after lunch. She had begun this ritual soon after Clara Belle's first appearance four years ago at the Miller Christmas breakfast.

"Just giving Mary Faith a break," she'd say if anyone in the family asked. Her motive was far deeper than that and she knew it. Both Mary Faith and Jordan were doing their part to encourage Clara Belle's potential academically and socially, but there were other crucial things only she could provide.

"Want to hear the song D-Doo-Dah taught me this week?" Clara Belle said as they walked into the parlor. The small room was located on the front corner of the large, old farm house. It was furnished wall to wall with Victorian chairs and sofas in various shades of crushed red velvet, vaguely resembling a miniature bordello. There was a walnut secretary on the back wall with glass doors and an intriguing number of diverse-sized drawers, obviously holding great secrets. On the front wall was a large bay window holding the remains of last year's, still-decorated, Christmas tree.

"Let's hear it," said Aunt Belle.

Clara Belle walked to the center of the room, cleared her throat and began,

"Oh where have you been, Billy Boy, Billy Boy?
Oh where have you been, charming Billy?
I have been to seek a wife, she's the joy of my life,
She's a young thing and cannot leave her mother."

"That's a good one…"

"I'm not finished yet; there are four more verses," which she commenced to sing in her unique alto voice, barely a breath in-between, and not a stutter in sight. She ended with her traditional "Ta-Dah."

"You're somethin', kid—you know that?" said Aunt Belle, applauding.

"Sure I d-do—you said so."

"Indeed I did. Now, you want to say the special words? Then we'll decide what we'll talk about today."

The two of them joined hands and repeated the exact words that Aunt Belle had whispered in her ear that first Christmas morning.

"Why d-do we say that every time?" Clara Belle asked, as she always did.

"You were born way too early. I don't know exactly when God gives a baby the soul He gives everyone—the unique soul that is just for that person. Since you had such a rough start in life and were working so hard just to survive, I thought you might need a little reminder of Who you belonged to," answered Aunt Belle, as she always did.

"Got any questions for me today? Then we'll memorize your Bible verses for Sunday school, and for a special treat I found a book at the library about China and some interesting fellows you'll never hear about at Garber's Church."

"China? Where's t...?"

"Questions first."

"What d-does retarded mean?" Clara Belle asked.

"Where'd you hear that?"

"Hank J-Jr."

"That little shit," she mumbled.

"He told D-Doo-Dah I was that."

"Well, he's wrong and so's anybody else you hear it from. That's an awful word that ignorant folks use for someone who learns slow. For sure, you aren't one of those, are you?"

"Nope."

"It's not even a nice word to use for people who are. I'll deal with Hank Jr. Did he ever say that to your face?"

"I just heard him tell D-Doo-Dah."

"If he ever does, tell him to…."

"Go to Hell?"

Aunt Belle stifled a laugh. "Maybe you'd better not put it quite that way."

"You and Uncle Henry d-do."

"That's different—we're old. Hey, I've got a new riddle for you. It's one us kids used to tell in the barn when we were growing up. Ready?"

"I was b-born ready."

"What's invisible and smells like carrots?"

"I don't know," said Clara Belle. "What's invisible and smells like carrots?"

"Bunny Farts! Ta-Dah!"

They both giggled until their stomachs hurt.

"OK," said Clara Belle, "now what ab-bout China?"

"Well, there were these three fellows, kind of like preachers who… "

~

As Clara Belle began to show that she could learn, and learn quickly, Ben Jr. became more accepting of her. He had withdrawn from Mary Faith and Clara Belle, embarrassed by his daughter's strange appearance and slow development. Everything changed when he realized how bright she was, and he began spending time with her, urging her on, hoping perhaps that she would outgrow her strangeness.

Jordan accepted Clara Belle without judgment; Clara Belle was Clara Belle and he loved her just the way she was. The Miller cousins' acceptance of her was based primarily on threats from their parents. "Don't let me ever hear you making fun of poor little Clara Belle," they were warned. With this option for interaction eliminated, the cousins simply ignored her. Jordan had accepted his role as Clara

Belle's teacher, protector and guardian and, as such, was also ignored.

Aunt Belle had told him that first Christmas morning that he would be her teacher, and that she would be his. At the time, Jordan was quite positive she had been mistaken about Clara Belle being *his* teacher.

Chapter 6

THE PROPHET SPEAKS

Jordan and Clara Belle attended Garber's Church, a Brethren church to which at least some of the Millers had belonged since their ancestors migrated from Pennsylvania to Virginia in the late 1700s. The tiny building had changed little since it was constructed in 1782. On either side of the center aisle, in a space smaller than most of the outbuildings on the farm, were eight or ten profoundly uncomfortable pine benches. In the sanctuary there were no stained-glass windows, no brass candlesticks, no organ and certainly no cross on the altar—to be precise, there was no altar, only a raised platform on which stood a wooden lectern used by the preacher. Plain and simple were the only furnishings permitted—anything remotely ornamental was considered idolatrous.

The congregation of Garber's Church, as in most Dunkard churches, was composed of good, solid folk who were fairly straight-laced and rarely got off their farms. They certainly had not encountered anyone like Clara Belle Miller. Church people are supposed to be sensitive and caring, especially adult church people. Sometimes they are not. When Jordan caught one of them staring rudely at Clara Belle, he walked up to them, put his hands on his hips and stared right back. Clara Belle soon learned the tactic and joined him. The offending person felt shamed enough by these brazen children that they ducked their heads and walked away. Jordan and Clara Belle were quite proud of the fact that they had outsmarted a grown-up.

The children at Sunday school and church choir were no problem. They thought Clara Belle was funny.

Clara Belle loved to sing, and at five years old her memory was phenomenal. While the rest of the children struggled for weeks to master the words, she could memorize every line of a song after the first rehearsal. This talent, plus the intriguing fact that she completely lost her stutter when she sang, amazed the other children. There was one problem—her voice stuck out like a sore thumb.

One Thursday after school Jordan and Clara Belle went to choir. Jordan sat next to her just in case she needed him for something.

"Our song for this week at church is 'All Creatures of our God and King,' " said Miss Etta, the choir director.

There was a titter of quiet voices of approval and then Clara Belle's loud whisper, "G-Goodie, my favorite."

"Not so loud, Clara Belle. Now, everyone sit up straight. Support your local voice."

Miss Etta lifted her hands to the piano keys and played the introduction. Nearing the end, she raised one hand to bring in the choir.

Twenty soprano voices, reasonably in tune, and one alto voice perfectly in tune, but a full octave lower than everybody else, began, "All Creatures of our God and King. Lift up your voice and let us sing, Alleluia."

Miss Etta raised her hand to stop them.

"Clara Belle, dear," Miss Etta said, "why don't you sing just a little bit quieter this time so we're all singing just alike."

The other children looked at Clara Belle, then at each other, stifling their giggles. Jordan squirmed in his seat.

"Now, children, settle down. Let's try it again."

"All creatures of our God and King," the choir of soprano voices began. Miss Etta smiled, pleased that her suggestion had coaxed Clara Belle's voice to blend with the other choristers. What she didn't know was that Clara Belle was mouthing the words, which lasted for only a few phrases.

"Lift up your voice and let US SING, A-L-L-E-LU-YA!!"
She couldn't help herself—the joy of the music and her en-
thusiasm for the words she sang soon overcame her and
she was again three times as loud as the other choir members. The same was true each time they sang another song
throughout the forty-five minute rehearsal.

"Let's try 'God Wants Me for a Sunbeam,' " said Miss
Etta. "Now, on this one, we want to use our sweetest sunbeam voices. One, two, three, one, two, sing."

"GOD WANTS ME FOR A STRING BEAN," sang Clara
Belle, full-throttle and with an absolutely straight face.

Jordan held his breath.

The rest of the choir dissolved into a chorus of snorts
and giggles and Miss Etta gave up.

"That's all the time we have for today—you are excused.
Be sure to be on time Sunday. Clara Belle, may I see you for
a minute?"

"I'll wait for you outside," said Jordan as he walked out
with the other children. He waited, biting his fingernails.

When she came out, she was smiling.

"How'd it go—did she give ya down the country?"

"Nah, D-Doo Dah. She likes me. She s-started laughing
as s-soon as everybody left."

"But don'cha feel bad when the other kids laugh at you
like that?"

"Why would I f-feel bad? I like making p-people laugh.
You just don't remember, I was born to love and I was b-
born to be funny."

After choir practice, when the children had gone home,
Miss Etta said to Mrs. Hartman, "What in heaven's name are
we going to do with Clara Belle in the Christmas pageant?"

There was no preparatory season for Christmas in the
Church of the Brethren—having Advent would have been
much too "Catholic." Not a single Christmas song was sung
before Christmas Eve and not one of them was heard after
the Sunday nearest Christmas Day. The only way to extend

the joyous season for Dunkards was to begin rehearsing the Christmas pageant immediately after Thanksgiving. As soon as the last of the turkey was made into hash, the time had come to cast the performance.

"No idea, Etta," said Mrs. Hartman, the pageant director. "She does love to sing but, well, you know… a non-speaking part, maybe?"

"She's only five, a little young for Mary. Angel?"

Mrs. Hartman grimaced.

"Guess not."

"If we let her sing in the choir, 'Silent Night' won't be the least bit silent and the Baby Jesus—well, He'd have to be way far away in the manger to get any sleep," laughed Miss Etta.

They pondered the dilemma.

"We could give her a verse or two from the Christmas story in Luke or maybe a little bit of Isaiah. Nobody'd have trouble hearing her," said Mrs. Hartman.

"That would work—how about the Angel Gabriel's announcement to Mary? All she has to say is, 'And behold you will conceive in your womb and bring forth a son and shall call his name Jesus.' She won't have any trouble memorizing that—what about the stuttering?"

"She doesn't stutter when she sings, maybe this will be the same. It's a chance we'll have to take," said Mrs. Hartman.

"Maybe she'd feel less nervous if we let Jordan be Joseph. He always takes up for her with the other children."

"And Mary?"

"LuEllen Heatwole looks the part but she's as mean as a snake—gives Jordan a hard time at choir. Maybe if we make her Mary, she'll rise to the occasion."

Jordan was a wreck. "LuEllen is taller and outweighs me by ten pounds," he told his mother. "I'm s'posed to stand there pretending to be Joseph, and the whole time I'm wondering if she's gonna give me noogie. And what about Clara Belle's speech? What if she starts stuttering?"

Rehearsals went perfectly and Clara Belle didn't miss a word. As with her singing, when she was in a performance mode and had an audience, she completely lost her stutter.

~Melinda~

I was ten that Christmas Eve. My Aunt Dorcas Deputy belonged to Garber's Church and invited me to come to the pageant. I had been reared as an Episcopalian and had never been in a Brethren church. As we sat down on one of the wooden benches with absolutely no padding like in my church, I glanced around. Most of the classrooms at my school were bigger. There was nothing remotely beautiful about the sanctuary—everything was plain and rather bleak.

"Are you sure this is a church?" I whispered.

"Shush, Melinda, they're getting ready to start."

Everyone took their places: the holy family, the shepherds, the angels and the choir. A spotlight was turned on that shined down on the right of the platform.

Then, I saw her.

She was tiny—all I could see at first was something that looked like a red clown wig. The strawberry-pink fluff bounced from side to side as she walked in front of the people on the first row toward the spotlight that waited for her. Someone helped her up and I realized that the back and forth motion of her head must be due to something wrong with her leg. When she turned around, I craned my neck to get a better look at her, and what I saw astounded me. I had never seen another little girl like her. Her eyes were huge and strangely shaped behind a pair of thick glasses, which were sliding down her nose. Even from where I was sitting I could see that her nose was covered with freckles. She looked around and grinned with a mouth that looked much too large for her face. She wore a white choir robe that was way too big—the sleeves made her hands and feet invisible. The spotlight shined on her wild hair and gave me the distinct impression that she had a halo. I looked in the program: "The prophet Isaiah—Clara Belle Miller."

The girl called Clara Belle paused. At first I thought she had forgotten what she was supposed to do, but then realized she was waiting to make certain she had everyone's attention. She started to speak. Her voice was coarse and low, not like a little girl's voice at all, and she began, "And behold you will conceive in your womb and bring forth a son and shall call his name Jesus," she paused.

A woman, who I guessed was the director, had been leaning forward, obviously anxious about what might happen. She relaxed, let out a big sigh and sat back in her pew. A very large man in a very large suit made his move to stand up. I assumed that this must be the minister, even though he wore no robe or anything else I was used to seeing a priest wear. But the girl was *not* finished. "Then a shoot shall grow from the stock of Jesse, and a branch shall spring from his roots," she continued. "The spirit of the Lord shall rest upon him, a spirit of wisdom and understanding, a spirit of counsel and power, a spirit of knowledge and the fear of the Lord…"

About then, I tuned out of her lengthy recitation and just stared—I couldn't figure out what it was about her. I had always been a pretty little girl, made over by my parents and family and accepted by my peers. How could this girl, weird-looking as she was, get up in front of everybody with such confidence? Didn't she know how she looked? Didn't she know what everybody was thinking? I couldn't be the only one that noticed.

"…The wolf shall live with the sheep and the leopard lie down with the kid; the calf and the young lion shall grow up together and a little child shall lead them."

The congregation sat dumbfounded. There was not a sound as we all watched her limp over to her pew and sit down. Her face was glowing and a little red and her slanted eyes were fiery. The preacher didn't move and looked precisely like a deer stuck immobile by headlights. He finally rose, coughed several times and began, "And it came to pass—"

The boy who was Joseph stared at Clara Belle from his post at the manger with a most un-Joseph-like expression. He watched her intently as she searched the audience, obviously looking for someone. Her gaze came to rest on a woman with henna-red hair, a very un-churchy dress and large dangly earrings. Slowly the little girl's smile started from her eyes, scrunching up her freckled nose, then her eyes; then the smile moved down to her mouth, turned up the corners, and she winked. The woman nodded her head and winked back. A young woman, maybe Clara Belle's mother, was beaming with pride; the man beside her was scrunching down in his pew, looking like he was trying to disappear, and beside me, my Aunt Dorcas whispered, "Melinda, I do believe that strange child is possessed."

Chapter 7

THE SOLUTION AND THE RIDDLE

Clara Belle looked in the full-length mirror on the bathroom door.

"Mommy, I like these pants best, d-don't you?"

"I think they're beautiful, sweetie, but are you sure that shirt and vest match?"

Clara Belle looked again. Her pants were purple with bright yellow sunflowers—more like pantaloons. Her mother had started making them when she was three and got her leg brace. Over one of Doo-Dah's hand-me-down T-shirts she had put on her favorite red and white polka dot vest.

"Sure they match, d-don't they, D-Daddy?"

Her father sat at the dining room table reading his newspaper. He peeked around the side, shook his head and frowned.

"Looks like something your Aunt Belle would put together."

"Aunt Belle's a g-gypsy goddess. See Mommy, D-Daddy likes it."

"I didn't mean... it's just not becoming, Clara Belle."

"What you have on is fine, Clara Belle," said her mother. "You ready to pick up Jordan and go up to Granddaddy's and hear a story while I go get some groceries?"

"I can't wait. D-Doo-Dah says Granddaddy tells the best and today he's going to t-tell us a big secret."

"Don't believe everything my father tells you. He stopped school when he was in sixth grade and has been on the farm all his life."

"Like your father says," said her mother, " 'schooling makes you no smarter than him, yet, more educated only.' "

"That's another thing; why can't he learn to speak English? He's a Virginian, not Pennsylvania Dutch."

"I like the way he talks," Clara Belle said as quietly as she could, hoping to stop her parents. She did this a lot. They always seemed to be yelling at each other about something. Most of the time it was about her.

"I've got to go teach a class. I'll probably be late for dinner; I have a meeting at 5:00."

He walked out the door.

"Bye, D-Daddy. Have a good day."

But he was already in the car.

"I know, Mommy, he's very b-busy."

"Let's go, Clara Belle."

They drove around the corner and beeped the horn at the Glick house. Jordan came running out.

"Hey, Clara Belle, you ready for a Granddaddy story?"

"She's ready, Jordan."

"I c-can answer myself, Mommy."

"Sorry, pumpkin, I just—"

"You get tired of waiting, just like D-Daddy."

"That's not so, Clara Belle. I—"

"Now, Clara Belle," said Jordan as the car turned around and headed up the lane, "you never know what story Granddaddy Miller's gonna tell, but you let me get him started and I betcha I can get him to tell us about our great-granddaddy and General Sheridan. That one's my favorite."

"What if I d-don't like that one?"

"You will, I promise, and if you don't, just wait till it's over; he'll have another one. Whatever you do, don't interrupt. He won't stop anyways till he's ready, and as soon as he finishes one story he starts the next one. And he'll always say, 'have I told you about such and such,' which is no problem for you since you've never heard any of his stories. But even if I've heard the one he's about to tell, I don't say nothin' 'cause he's gonna tell it anyways."

They climbed the long hill, and then went down the other side as Granddaddy's white, frame house came into view. As they pulled up to the gate, they heard a loud scream. Clara Belle jumped and looked toward the noise. There, strutting up to the barn in full spread was Granddaddy's peacock, Moses.

"Don't be scared, Clara Belle, he just makes a lot of noise—he won't hurt you."

"I already knew that."

"OK, kids, you go on in. I'll be back in about an hour. Be good and don't bother Grandmother Miller. She's not feeling too well."

"That's just her excuse for being so mean," said Jordan. "My mom says when her real mother died, this Grandmother Miller used to chase her and Aunt Belle around with a broom."

"Jordan, enough of that—she does the best she can. Now, if I'm a little late, don't you go off somewhere—just sit there on the steps and wait."

They hopped out of the car and opened the iron gate.

"You know, Clara Belle, my mom said when she first started to drive, she was already to choir practice at church when Granddaddy called Miss Etta and told her to tell Mom to get herself home right now, she forgot to shut this very gate and she---"

"D-Doo-Dah, I want to hear Granddaddy's stories, not yours."

The front door of the big white house was on a high porch. There were two flights of stairs, one on each end of the porch. The space underneath the porch was covered with lattice-work and was one of the best hiding places at Granddaddy's.

"When Granddaddy first brought Grandmother Miller home, all the kids hid—"

"Doo-Dah!"

"OK, but you're missing a good one."

44

They climbed the stairs and Jordan knocked on the door—nothing. He knocked again, a little harder—still nothing.

"He's prob'ly asleep on the couch and Grandmother Miller is deaf as a post. I know they're home."

Just as he started to hit the door one more time, Grandmother Miller came to the door with a nasty frown.

"What in heaven's name do you want?" she said. "Granddaddy's asleep—now go on home."

"No, no, Mother," came a voice from the living room. "Who ist?"

"Me and Clara Belle," Jordan yelled from the door where their large grandmother blocked the way.

"Come in you nit-wit kids and have a sitz. Mother, let them in, yet."

Clara Belle looked up at Grandmother Miller looming in the doorway. She waited until Doo-Dah took her hand and they walked right past to the sofa where Granddaddy lay, very much awake.

"Well now, Jordan, where found you this little kid with the stribbley red hairs?" asked Granddaddy Miller.

"I'm Clara B-Belle Miller and I'm not little, I'm f-four and three-quarters," said Clara Belle, pulling herself up as straight as she could.

"Well, well, I'll be switched; you are pretty big for sure. Why do you two come up here to see your old grandfatter?"

"Doo-Dah says you tell good stories about the b-barn and I want to hear one."

"You told her this, Jordan? Well, I guess I might have one or two. Have I told you the one about how General Sheridan comes down the valley burning barns?"

Doo-Dah smiled at her and then motioned for her to sit down by the sofa.

"It was because my grandfatter was a good man that General Sheridan didn't burn our barn by the Civil War. When the Union army comes down south to our valley, some soldiers end up having dinner here in this house. Millers are from back aways keepers of the peace. The first Miller, Hans Benjamin Mueller, comes here to keep his three sons out the army of Chermany."

"What's the army of Cher—"

"Clara Belle," Doo-Dah whispered, shaking his head, "don't interrupt, remember?"

"How Grandfatter came to having soldiers in his own house, this is a puzzlement. They are watching Grandfatter going to the wash house; he fills the wagon up with food and makes off to deliver it to some poor peoples by Dayton. He comes back, makes a sitz at the table with the union soldiers and prays to the Lord a long Dunkard prayer for the vittles. He makes eating and talking with the union soldiers, then reads from the Holy Bible. All these things, I reckon, makes these men of war think once again about burning our barn. They make tracks down the lane and the best I know, never come back. Listen up, Chordan and Clara Belle!" he said. Clara Belle knew this was the important part.

"Sitzing down at table with your enemies is not just a suggestion; it is a solution."

Clara Belle was having more than a little trouble following the story. The more he talked the more funny words he used that she hadn't heard before. But she didn't say anything because just being there with Granddaddy was fun.

They waited for the next story, but Granddaddy was finished.

"Skedaddle you two shite-pokes, time for my schnooz."

"But Granddaddy, what about the b-big secret? Doo-Dah said you'd t-tell us."

"He did, did he? Well, I don't want to make a lie. But only a hint today. Something in the barn is. Very old, very old. Like a treasure, yet."

He shut his eyes and didn't say another word.

They looked around for Grandmother Miller, but she had gone back to the kitchen.

They let themselves out the front door and both looked up at the barn.

"Let's g-go see."

"Your mom said not to go anywhere. She'll get mad."

"She won't know. We'll just s-stay a little bit. Besides, you said when I was b-bigger you'd take me inside. I'm bigger."

"Well, all right, but just for a minute. Your mom'll be back soon."

They walked up the gravel road to the old barn and tried to imagine the soldiers standing right there, deciding whether or not to burn it.

"I'm glad they didn't."

Clara Belle nodded, knowing exactly what he meant.

Moses screeched at them again, but this time Clara Belle was ready.

"You are very b-beautiful Moses; now shut up."

As they reached the large double doors of the barn, Doo-Dah said, "Let me go in first, just in case."

"Just in c-case, what?"

"You never know what you're gonna meet in a barn."

"You're j-just trying to scare me."

"Am not—let me look in first."

She watched Doo-Dah slide the big white door and look into the huge dark space inside. There was a flutter of surprised pigeons. Doo-Dah slid open the other door and the dark barn flooded with light.

"OK, Clara Belle, it's safe."

She looked around the enormous building. She had heard her daddy talk about how he and his sisters used to play in this barn. They had played hide-and-seek mostly. She looked for the long rope that hung from the very top where they would swing from one side of the hayloft to the other and drop in the hay—it was still there. There was something else Aunt Belle said they did, but she couldn't remember.

"Clara Belle, how 'bout the treasure? Wanna look around a little?"

"Sure, I g-guess," she said, but she was thinking about something else.

They looked in the tool room and under some piles of hay in the corner.

Clara Belle walked across the barn floor away from Doo-Dah. She happened to look up at the light coming in the window way at the top. She suddenly remembered the other thing Aunt Belle had said her sisters did.

"I gotta d-do something."

Before he could stop her, she was climbing, brace and all, up the ladder to the hayloft.

"Clara Belle, you come down right now. You're gonna kill yourself and then your mom'll kill me for not taking good care of you."

"Don't worry, D-Doo-Dah—I'm just fine—you s-stay right there."

She walked to the exact spot where the dusty sunbeam shone just right on her frizzy strawberry head. She fixed her costume so it looked perfect. She looked down to make sure Doo-Dah was paying attention there on the barn floor below. Then she said in her best loud voice,

"Hey, Doo-Dah, what's invisible and smells like carrots?"

Chapter 8

THE GYPSY GODDESS

Aunt Belle stood in her messy kitchen mixing up the potato salad for the Miller Easter picnic. She was already late because she had been trying a new color on her hair and it went a shade too black. She added some of the auburn she used last month, which took awhile to set. She'd looked in the mirror and liked what she saw. Of course, then it had been necessary to change to a completely different outfit that accentuated her new "do." Finally, she had gone rooting in her jewelry box and dug out the dangly rhinestone earrings she had found at Glen's Fairprice the week before.

"Damn, you look good—like a gypsy goddess," said Uncle Henry, coming into the kitchen with an admiring smile.

"She get that from you? Sounds like Clara Belle."

There was a long pause before he said, "Think she'll ever be normal?"

"Jeezy-peezy, now you sound like my sisters—worse yet, her father. She's normal—just different. You'd think after all the time they spent wait'n for a baby, he'd be glad to have'er."

"Y' know Ben Jr. Since he went off and got all that education he thinks he's better'n the rest of you."

"Just 'cause he's a college professor doesn't mean he's not ever gonna step in another pile of cow shit. Now go get the kids, we're late."

He walked to the screen door.

"Hank Jr., Susan, time to go," Uncle Henry called.

The two of them came running out of the old wash house in the back that had become their playhouse.

Aunt Belle watched out the window as Uncle Henry put out his cigarette and started up the car. He loved this latest one and so did the kids because of the rumble seat. They jumped in the back and waited for their mother.

"Hurry up, Mom, we won't have enough time to swing on the barn rope," yelled Hank Jr. as she came out the porch door with the bowl of potato salad.

They drove the twenty-minute drive to the Miller farm. They weren't the last ones there—Aunt Clara and Uncle Mike always had that honor.

The children got out of the car and went straight up to the barn. Uncle Henry looked for his smoking buddies out back and Aunt Belle went inside.

The men had set up the picnic table by the fish pond. Most of the food was already there and, like Christmas morning, there was a lot of it: sliced ham and turkey, bean salad, potato salad, Jell-O-cottage cheese salad and tossed salad. There were deviled eggs, pickled eggs and egg salad. Aunt Belle looked to see if anyone had made smearcase— usually Kate made it because you had to use unpasturized milk straight from the barn. She finally saw the dish down with all the desserts, and next to it were the homemade strawberry preserves.

"Ring the bell for the kids—think they're all up at the barn," she said. "And go in and tell Daddy we're ready for the blessing."

Aunt Bootie went over to the bell, which had called the family together for four generations. She rang it three or four times and the children came running down from the barn, laughing and whispering among themselves. They were pointing to Clara Belle, who was tagging along behind with Jordan helping her down the hill—Aunt Belle took note. The cousins, especially her own son, gave Clara Belle a pretty hard time, even though all the parents had threatened them within an inch of their lives not to tease her. Then she saw Clara Belle's face. It was glowing, a little like at the

Christmas pageant—that performance had been a surprise to everyone except Aunt Belle. Jordan, too, was sporting a satisfied grin. As always he was Clara Belle's protector—Aunt Belle had seen to that on their first Christmas morning at Granddaddy Miller's.

"Fatter in heaven," her father had begun grace. "We thank you for this fine family who gets together here this day. We are blessed with many things, this farm, this house and all the childrens. Bless these vittles to our bodies and our lives to Thy service. Amen."

Granddaddy and Grandmother Miller went through the line first and back into the house to eat. The children who could fill their plates themselves were next, then the parents who had young children, and then anyone who was left.

Aunt Belle saw Susan, Hank Jr. and Jordan on the ledge of the fish pond, but no Clara Belle. She went inside to see if Granddaddy and Grandmother needed anything and found Clara Belle whispering in Granddaddy's ear.

Granddaddy called her over, "Belle, after eating, we have something special from our kleine clown." He winked at Clara Belle—she winked back at him and then at Aunt Belle.

Aunt Belle went back outside and announced, "OK everybody, when you finish your dessert, come on in the house—Granddaddy Miller has something to say."

The children quickly climbed the front steps, crashed through the front door into the front hall and lined up on the stairs, hoping Granddaddy had a good story. The adults sat where they could in the living room and spilled out into the hall and dining room—Granddaddy and Grandmother were at their places in front of the fireplace.

"We have a special treat this day. Little Clara Belle—"

"I'm n-not little, I'm five," came a croaky voice from the stairs.

"Scuse me—big Clara Belle will now give us her joke."

Clara Belle climbed down off the second step and walked into the living room. There was tittering from the other cousins, and when Jordan joined Clara Belle, Aunt Belle saw the look on his face and she froze. She had a very bad feeling about this but she couldn't do anything now.

Clara Belle's outfit was somewhat clownish as always, but for family gatherings Mary Faith prevailed in choosing her clothes. Her pantaloons were pink with white daisies; her blouse was white with a fluffy collar made of the print in her pants. She did have on the red and white polka dot vest which she had obviously hidden away and pulled out for this occasion.

"This is 'specially f-for my Daddy."

Ben Jr. stood in the doorway to the outside porch.

"Here goes."

"Hey, Doo-Dah, what's invisible and smells like carrots?"

Jordan hesitated.

The cousins on the stairs were bent over laughing.

"Come on, Doo-Dah," she whispered.

He swallowed and delivered his line, "I don't know, Clara Belle, what's invisible and smells like carrots?"

There was a pause, and then, in her booming voice, she said, "BUNNY FARTS—TA-DAH!"

Clara Belle's arms shot up in the air. She smiled from ear to ear and then looked at her father.

Aunt Belle looked, too, and her heart sank.

There was a huge silence as everyone looked from one to the other, not quite knowing what to do.

There were a few snorts from the uncles.

Aunt Lillian's face turned white.

Granddaddy looked at Grandmother. "How's about that, this kleine clown, she didn't make stuttering."

Mary Faith put her hands over her face and Ben Jr. came storming into the room and grabbed Clara Belle by the arm.

"Don't you know any better than that?" He picked her up and stomped out the front door with Mary Faith running after him.

"But, D-Daddy..." she heard Clara Belle cry.

Aunt Belle sat down on the sofa and tears stung her eyes. She knew how Clara Belle felt. She'd been there before—many times.

Chapter 9

THE SNIPING CAPER

"Well, yes, Belle," Jordan heard his mother talking on the phone, "I did think he over-reacted to the Easter joke thing."

He always eavesdropped when he knew someone was talking about Clara Belle, especially when there was something going on.

"—yesterday. Seemed OK to me.

"Well, maybe—

"Now, Belle, don't—

"All I said to her was, 'It's just not becoming, Clara Belle.'

"Now don't get in a snit, Belle, we're all trying, you know.

"Belle, stop cursing, you know I hate that.

"All right, let's just drop it. You said you had two things to talk about.

"Sure, I'll ask him—

"Aunt Belle's on the phone, Jordan," yelled his mother. "She wants to know if you and Clara Belle want to come up to spend the night tonight and tomorrow up at her house."

"You kiddin', you know we do. Tell'er yes quick before she changes her mind."

"I guess you heard that, Belle. I'll check with Mary Faith and call you back—

"No, I'm not going to ask; I'm sure she's fine. Call you back in a minute. Bye."

She hung up the phone and turned to Jordan.

"Jordan, has Clara Belle said anything about her joke at the picnic?"

Jordan thought for a minute. He didn't see Clara Belle as much now, being in third grade and having farm chores after school. He still saw her at church choir on Thursdays and on weekends up at the barn or like this weekend, going up to Aunt Belle and Uncle Henry's.

"Nope, now call Aunt Mary Faith and ask."

"Excuse me?"

"Please."

"Better."

His mother waited for the operator. "Yes, Maude, 43217, please…, thank you."

"Hello, Mary Faith—Kate."

"Just fine, thanks."

Jordan saw his mother holding the telephone away from her ear as Aunt Mary Faith went on and on.

"Well, you know how my brother is sometimes…I suppose so… Well, listen Mary Faith, Belle called and wants the kids to come up tonight and stay over tomorrow. I can take them up…OK, I'll wait."

Jordan stood staring into the refrigerator, waiting.

"Close the door…, Yes, Mary Faith.

"That's exactly what Jordan said. I'll call her back and pick up Clara Belle in about half an hour. By the way…Oh never mind. Be over in awhile. Bye."

To Jordan, a half hour waiting to go to Aunt Belle's was forever. Finally, his mother said, "Ready, Jordan?"

"You kiddin'?"

"Don't get smart, young man."

They got in the car and drove to the little house.

Before Jordan even got to the stoop, he heard Clara Belle and her mother.

"How 'bout I fix your hair in ponytails?"

"What's the use? My stupid hair won't s-stay in the rubber bands more than t-two seconds anyways."

He knocked on the screen door.

"Come on in, D-Doo-Dah. I'm almost ready."

"Let's go, Clara Belle. Mom's got the car all warmed up and we want to have plenty of time in the wash house before it gets dark."

"Daddy will be disappointed not to see you when he gets home from work," said Aunt Mary Faith.

Clara Belle turned around and gave her mother the strangest look.

"Let's go, Doo-Dah," she said, and they ran to the car. Even with her brace, Clara Belle could keep up with him now.

Aunt Mary Faith yelled from the porch, "Have a good time and you be good now."

Again, the look.

~

The ride to Hinton always seemed to take forever. Waiting for them was Aunt Belle and Uncle Henry's white-frame farmhouse. It was large, comfortable, and messy, with tucked-away secret rooms that inspired childhood imaginations to great adventures. Since Aunt Belle never threw anything away, there were trunks and bureaus full of old stuff for games and dress-up. Of course, the girls liked that more than Jordan and Hank Jr.

When they finally got there, they jumped out of the car without so much as a so-long to their chauffeur.

Aunt Belle met them at the door.

"Where are Susan and Hank Jr.?" asked Jordan.

"Already in the wash house waiting—got a Fresh Air kid, too. Go on out—I'll call you in when supper's ready."

They headed to the wash house. The inside was a lot better than the one at Granddaddy Miller's because Susan and Hank Jr. had it stocked with stuff for everything they could think up to play.

"Jordan, Clara Belle, this is Erik—he's from New York City."

The dark-complexioned boy nodded at them both, and then took an extra look at Clara Belle.

"Hi, Jordan," said Hank Jr. "Hello, brain-fart."

"Hello, turd-head."

"Good, very good," said Hank Jr. "Where'd you get that one?"

"Your m-mom."

"Enough, you two," said Susan. "We're going to play doctor and patient first." She was oldest, so she got to pick the game.

"Do we have to?" asked Jordan, who always ended up being the patient who had to take the "medicines" his two older cousins had concocted. The shelves were lined with bottles that they had taken empty from Aunt Belle's kitchen. They had been washed and filled with "doctored" water for playing doctor and patient. You never knew what they had put in them from the spice cabinet. If the patient was lucky, the medicine prescribed by Dr. Hank might taste like vanilla or mint, but more often than not, he or nurse Susan chose the one mixed with vinegar, hot pepper or worse.

"I'd rather play school," he said. "Susan, you're such a great teacher."

Susan considered this for a moment.

"Well, OK," said Susan, "but just for a little while."

A relieved Jordan and the rest of them headed to the corner of the wash house that was used as the school. There was a blackboard, a teacher's desk and a couple of chairs for students. They had saved old textbooks from school and Hank Jr. and Susan found supplies needed for teacher and pupils in Uncle Henry's office: paper, pencils, paper clips, clipboards and, when Uncle Henry wasn't looking, nabs and Pepsis from the employees' lounge.

"All right students, please sit in your seats. Erik, you sit there. Take out your pencil and paper and we're going to do arithmetic first."

Jordan hated arithmetic but kept his mouth shut—he'd rather do that than take his chances on doctor and nurse.

School lasted until it started to get dark and they heard Aunt Belle ringing the supper bell. Jordan had escaped today, but he knew tomorrow was another day—sooner or later, he'd have to take his medicine.

"What are we having for d-dinner, Aunt Belle?" asked Clara Belle as they ran into the kitchen.

"Jesse's hot dogs with everything, potato chips and ice cream," Aunt Belle announced, flipping a dishtowel in the air.

"You're the best cook ever, Aunt Belle; I wish I could eat here every meal," said Jordan.

Immediately after supper, they cleared the dining room table and set up the Monopoly game.

Aunt Belle brought in a bowl of popcorn, some fudge brownies with nuts and bottles of Pepsi and said, "Don't stay up too late," which meant absolutely nothing—at Aunt Belle's they could stay up as late as they wanted.

Clara Belle was still too young to actually play by herself so she was Susan's assistant.

"I want my own p-piece this time—the little shoe."

"OK," said Susan, "but you can't play for real. You can roll the dice and move your shoe but you can't have any money or buy anything."

"C-Can't I have just a little money for pretend?"

"Oh, for crab's sake," said Hank Jr., "can we get this game started? Clara Belle's gonna ruin the whole thing. She's such a looney-tunes."

"And you're a p-piss ant."

"You kids clean up your damn language," said Uncle Henry from the next room.

"Which token do you want?' asked Hank Jr., looking at Erik.

He shrugged, "Don't much care. Never played."

"Never p-played, why—"

"How about the car—that all right? And you can be my partner," said Hank Jr.

Erik nodded, picked up his token, organized his money, and didn't say another word for the rest of the game— not that he had much of a chance.

The game finally ended about 12:30 A.M. Clara Belle had fallen asleep around 10:00 and Uncle Henry carried her up to bed. Susan had won, as usual, owning hotels on Park Place, Boardwalk and all the utilities plus everybody else's money, including Clara Belle's "pretend." The boys were humiliated that a girl had once again beaten them.

They headed up the stairs for bed, passing the parlor where Aunt Belle's Christmas tree stood, still fully decorated—it would be there until Halloween. The parlor was also the place where Clara Belle and Aunt Belle had special conferences. Jordan didn't know what they talked about, but when Clara Belle came out, she limped a little less and stood a little taller.

Jordan was so high on the caffeine from Pepsi and brownies he couldn't go to sleep—and, of course, there was *the plan*—could they still do it with Erik around? "Got everything ready for tomorrow, Hank Jr.?" he said, but his cousin was already asleep.

~

"It's already nine o'clock—g-get up!" yelled Clara Belle as she charged into their room and leaped onto the bed. That was another great thing about Aunt Belle's—no matter how late you stayed up, you could sleep the next morning.

They dressed and went downstairs to the kitchen.

"Where we goin' today?" asked Jordan.

"I can't go anywhere," said Susan. "I have to do my 4-H project."

"Come on, Susan, can't you d-do it later?"

"Nope, record book's due Monday night. You go ahead with the boys."

Hank Jr. looked over at Jordan and winked.

"How 'bout the dump behind Mr. Foley's place?" said Hank Jr. "Let's see what we can dig up. I saw a big truck go over that way yesterday with a load of stuff—pickings ought to be great. Erik, you'll love this place."

"Eat first—you need a healthy breakfast," said Aunt Belle as she set out the glazed donuts and chocolate milk. "Sandwiches to go—what kind?"

"I want peanut butter, banana and mayonnaise," said Jordan.

"Me t-too," said Clara Belle.

"Me too," said Hank Jr. "You, Erik?"

"I—"

"Bananas will go brown," said Susan.

"Miss know-it-all," said Hank Jr.

"Just trying to be a help."

"Butt out."

"What about baloney and cheese?" asked Jordan.

Aunt Belle opened the meat drawer in the refrigerator and pulled out an unwrapped pile of something green.

"G-Gross."

"Like your baloney green, I can fill your order. I got cheese or—"

"Just peanut butter and mayonnaise for me and Erik," said Hank Jr. He stuck out his tongue at Susan.

"No bananas for us either," Jordan said.

"I'll talk for me, thank you v-very much—I'll have cheese and m-mustard, please."

Jordan shrugged, "Suit yourself."

"Kids, I have to go into town to take this stew to the Salvation Army. Uncle Henry'll be here if you need anything."

After about a half-hour hike over the hill and past Mr. Foley's farm, they reached the dump. They scanned the huge pile of junk.

"Looks like my neighborhood," said Erik, looking around.

"New stuff's over there," Hank Jr. said, pointing to a fresh pile of junk that had been dumped the day before. This was not a dump for regular household garbage; that was burned by each farm family in a nearby field. This was a sinkhole full of treasure: old furniture, broken dishes and milk crocks, and other household items that could be carted back to the wash house.

"How 'bout this old churn? Jar's broken, but we could use the paddle for something at the hospital, like maybe an operation," said Hank Jr., smiling wickedly. Jordan cringed.

"Here's an old file cabinet," said Jordan. "Be great to put the school stuff in."

"How'd we c-carry it back, you dummy?"

"Dad's pickup, fart-head," said Hank Jr.

"You know your dad says 'if you can't c-carry it, you don't need it.' "

They continued their search.

"Would you t-take a look at this?" Clara Belle said.

The three boys walked over to where she stood staring at something sticking out from the heap of trash.

"An old-lady shoe—big deal," said Hank Jr.

"It's attached to something. How creepy is that?" said Jordan.

"What the he...?" said Erik.

"Well, I'm n-not afraid," said Clara Belle as she grabbed hold of the black-laced, high-top shoe.

"Help me, D-Doo-Dah—it's stuck."

"Not willing to lose face, Jordan grasped the area above the shoe and both of them tugged. Whatever it was suddenly let go, throwing both Jordan and Clara Belle to the ground. Clara Belle lay flat, holding the object straight up in the air.

"Gross," said Hank Jr. "It's some old lady's wooden leg."

"Who c-could this belong to?" said Clara Belle, already concocting a good story about it. "Do either of you know s-somebody around here with a wooden leg? And why would she throw it away?"

"Put it back," said Hank Jr. "It gives me the cree—"

"Maybe someone murdered the old lady and threw the leg away so there wouldn't be any clues," suggested Jordan.

"Let's take it b-back to the wash house and start an investigation about it," said Clara Belle. "We can ask Aunt B-Belle and Uncle Henry—they know everybody around here. This c-could be really exciting."

Hank Jr. glanced at Jordan and nodded his head.

"You know what's even more exciting is that I heard there are snipes around this dump."

"Snipes, w-what's that?"

"You never heard of snipes?" joined Jordan. "It's a small animal that lives around dumps and if you catch them you can sell them to the… the —"

"To the Forestry Department—they like people to round them up."

"Are they dangerous?" asked Erik.

"Not if you catch them right and keep them in the bag." He pulled out an old feed sack from his backpack.

"How much d-do you get?"

"Oh, prob'ly five dollars a snipe."

"Let's try to catch one. How d-do we do it?"

"Not hard at all," said Hank Jr. "You take this bag and hold it open. Us boys will go off and try to scare one up. You just stand here with the bag and yell 'here snipe, here snipe' and when he runs up you catch him and shut the bag real fast, because they're quick as lightning."

"How come I c-can't scare one up and one of you hold the bag?"

" 'Cause, you don't know where they hide," said Jordan. "Hank Jr. and I do. You have the most important job anyways."

"Whatever you do," said Hank Jr., "don't move from where you are. We'll head the snipe your way. You ready?"

"I was b-born ready. Here snipe, here snipe!"

Jordan, Hank Jr. and Erik ran off into the woods next to the dump, banging on a tin can with a stick, stifling their laughter as long as they could.

"You sure she can find her way home?" said Jordan, suddenly feeling a little guilty.

"Sure, she's been here a dozen times."

In the distance, they could hear Clara Belle, "Here snipe, here snipe!"

"She's really into it now—she's not even stuttering," said Jordan. "Let's go down to the creek and catch some craw-dads."

"I don't get it," said Erik.

"Come on with us, we'll tell you. I guess they don't have snipe hunts in the city," he laughed.

They stayed at the creek for about a half-hour and had no luck. They did catch some tadpoles, which they put in the tin can with some water. Then they sat down and ate their sandwiches.

"She's probably figured out we tricked her by now," said Hank Jr. "Let's go back to the house and have a good laugh. She'll be so pissed."

They circled back past the dump—Clara Belle was nowhere to be seen.

"Good, let's go," said Jordan.

They walked back to Aunt Belle's. Jordan's mother was already there waiting to pick them up.

"Now I'm in trouble—my mom won't think this is that funny."

Aunt Belle met them at the door.

"Where's Clara Belle?" she asked.

"She isn't here yet?" said Hank Jr.

"What do you mean? She's supposed to be with you boys."

Jordan and Hank Jr. looked at each other.

"Uh, we sort of…uh, well, we sort of played the snipe trick on her," said Hank Jr.

"You what?" asked Jordan's mother.

"Well, yeah," said Jordan. "Smart as she is, we figured she'd be back by now—wouldn't take her long to figure out—"

"I cannot believe you did that," said Aunt Belle. "Good Lord, she's only five. Boys, you are in deep trouble. Get right out there and try to find her. We'll stay here just in case she comes back to the house—beginning to look wooly."

She looked at the sky as lightning flashed, followed by a quick boom of thunder.

Jordan's heart was in his throat and he felt sick to his stomach.

"Let's go, Hank Jr.; we gotta find her."

The three of them headed back toward the dump.

"I can't believe you talked me into this," Jordan said.

"Did not."

"Did too—you said she'd be all right. If something happens to her, I…I—" He was very close to tears.

For an hour they looked everywhere. All they found was the snipe sack at the dump. It had begun to rain. They looked for footprints, but there were none—the rain had washed them away. Both of them were in a panic and soaked to the skin.

"We can't go back until we find her," said Jordan. "Aunt Mary Faith will never forgive me—I'm supposed to… Please God, let her be all right," he said, looking up at the dark, thundering sky.

"We better go back and get some help looking," said Hank Jr.

They ran back to the house, dreading telling the adults that they hadn't found Clara Belle. Aunt Belle and Jordan's mom were waiting on the back porch.

"Well…?" said Aunt Belle.

"We didn't find her," said Hank Jr. "We came back to get help looking. Mom, we're really sorry."

"Let me get my raincoat," said Aunt Belle, as she headed into the house.

As the boys stood waiting and dripping on the back porch, Jordan's mother glared at him—he'd never felt so scared in his life.

"TA-Dah!" came the familiar voice from inside the kitchen.

With a flourish and a self-satisfied grin, Aunt Belle opened the screen door. There stood Clara Belle, arms extended above her head, triumphantly clutching the wooden leg by its old-lady shoe.

"Bet your b-boots there'll be a great story about this caper," she said, walking out on the porch. "*Now* who's the fart-head?"

Chapter 10

THE FAMILY TREASURE

Her sixth birthday was today.

Clara Belle had already figured out they were planning a surprise party. She had heard her mother talking on the phone with Aunt Belle and Aunt Kate, and Doo-Dah kept dropping hints. But she didn't let on that she knew and she was a little bit sorry she'd found out. A surprise would have been fun and it was hard work pretending you didn't know.

"Clara Belle, it's time to go into Jesse's Lunch and get a hot dog and then we'll do a little shopping at Glen's Fairprice for something for your birthday."

"Can D-Doo-Dah come?"

"Not this time. I think he's busy helping his mom up at the barn today."

Another clue, she thought.

"All right, I'm ready. Is D-Daddy going?"

"No, honey, he has to work."

"Like always."

"He'll be back later for the... He'll be back a little later."

Clara Belle smiled.

They went to town, got a hot dog and fries at Jesse's Lunch, then went to Glen's Fairprice at the end of Main Street. This was Clara Belle's favorite store—it had everything you could imagine. Toys, books, gadgets of every kind, and everything was piled up on top of everything else so you had to sift through it to find the really good stuff.

"I want this b-book of jokes and riddles," she said.

"Let me look at it first and make sure they're becoming for your age."

Her mother gave her one of her looks.

"Aunt Belle t-told me the bunny one."

"Well, I'll have to have a talk with Aunt Belle."

They paid for the book, went to the car and started for home. She saw her mother looking at her watch.

They stopped at the little house and went in.

"Come in your room; I have a little surprise for you."

There on the bed was a clown outfit, just her size. It was bright red with yellow yarn pompoms down the front. The fluffy clown collar was yellow, too. There was a red pointy clown hat with a big yellow pompom to match the ones on the suit.

"Oh, Mommy, it's b-beautiful. Thank you, thank you."

"Why don't you try it on and then we'll go up to Granddaddy's and show him and Grandmother."

She put on the outfit and looked in the mirror—she looked like a real clown.

"Let me p-pick out a joke from my new book. Read me a g-good one."

Mary Faith leafed through the book. "Here's one— knock, knock."

"Who's there?"

"Cowsgo."

"Cowsgo, who?"

"No they don't, they go moo."

Clara Belle laughed. "I like that," she said. "I like the bunny-fart one better," she mumbled.

"What?"

"Nothing," said Clara Belle.

"Ready?"

She looked in the mirror and did the knock-knock joke again with her mother.

"I was b-born ready."

"Don't be smart," her mother said, along with the *look*.

They drove up the hill and down the other side. She kept going over the joke in her head so she wouldn't forget. Maybe Daddy would like this one better and she wouldn't get spanked.

They drove right by Granddaddy's house and up to the barn.

Both barn doors opened and out piled a crowd of kids and grown-ups yelling "Surprise! Surprise!"—and she was surprised.

The theme was everything circus. A table was carried out of the barn with plates, cups and paper napkins with clowns on them. The cake was in the shape of a circus tent, and when Aunt Belle came out of the barn with a whole handful of balloons, Clara Belle saw that she wore a clown costume exactly like hers.

"Ta-Dah, Happy Birthday, shite-poke, now ain't we somethin'?"

Everyone had on some kind of circus costume from animals to performers. Doo-Dah walked up wearing jeans, a shirt with a string tie, a cowboy hat and boots.

"What are you supposed to be, D-Doo-Dah?"

"Cowboy. What's it look like?"

"There are no c-cowboys in a circus."

"Look, Clara Belle, I'm not about to wear some stupid costume, not even for you. Just be glad I'm here. I have other things to do besides—"

"That'll do, Jordan," said Aunt Belle.

Uncle Henry dragged out five or six chicken coops with different animals in them: Jordan's little sister Emily's two cats, some peepeys, six rabbits, one rooster and a baby pig. They lined up the coops outside the barn to look like circus cages. Uncle Fred had trucked over three ponies from his farm for the children to ride, and Jordan and his dad had pitched extra hay in the loft for dropping off the barn swing.

All of the Miller aunts, uncles and cousins were there, as well as the farm hands and their children. Aunt Mary Faith had also invited some of Jordan and Clara Belle's friends from Sunday school and church choir.

Clara Belle looked around the group and finally saw what she was looking for.

"Daddy, you c-came, you came!" She ran toward him.

"Don't fall down, Clara Belle, you'll get your new outfit all dirty."

"I've g-got a new joke. Mommy picked it out. Ready?"

He looked at Mary Faith—she nodded her head.

"Go ahead, then."

"Knock, knock."

"Who's there?"

"Cowsgo."

"Cowsgo, who?"

"No they don't, they go moo. TA-DAH!"

Ben Jr. smiled and said, "Much better, Clara Belle, much better." Then he turned and walked over to the food table to get a Pepsi.

"He liked it, Aunt B-Belle—you see him smile?"

"Humph," said Aunt Belle.

What everybody liked most was in the barn.

Clara Belle went inside, hoping her mother would let her do the swing today since she was six.

She watched as one of the farm boys climbed up the ladder to the hayloft, holding the fat hemp rope, which hung from the very top beam of the barn. Another boy, already in the hayloft, held the rope steady, while the "swinger" hopped on the knot he could reach. When he was ready he yelled, "Geronimo," and the holder let him go. Over her head he flew, all the way to the other hayloft, where he dropped into the hay.

"Mommy, can I—?"

"May I, Clara Belle, may I."

"May I?"

"Not yet," said her mother.

"B-But I'm six now."

"You're too little and your brace will get in the way."

"B-But M—"

"No buts about it—when you're a little older, maybe. Now go on outside and play with the other kids."

She stomped out of the barn. "I can't ever d-do anything fun."

Aunt Belle was just coming in.

"Come with me, shite-poke, let's go look for secret treasure," she said and led her down toward Granddaddy's house.

"But Granddaddy said the t-treasure was in the barn."

"Used to be—I moved it when I was ten."

Aunt Belle led Clara Belle past the fishpond and opened the door to the old wash house. This wash house was a little creepy because it hadn't been made into a playhouse like at Aunt Belle's. There was a big stone fireplace with an iron pot hanging where Granddaddy Miller told them his Grandmother had cooked for the family a long time ago. There was some junky furniture and boxes filled with old papers from Granddaddy's office. In the corner was an old pump organ that still played if you had strong enough legs.

Aunt Belle reached behind the organ and pulled out a box. The rusted tin container was about the size of a child's shoebox and was handmade. It had a domed lid, held in place by a heavy metal latch. On the front was the faint outline of a flowered design and flecks of what had been red paint.

"Is the t-treasure inside that box?"

"Yep," said Aunt Belle.

She very carefully lifted the lid of the tin box—Clara Belle craned her neck to see what was inside.

Chapter 11

THE PARLOR TALK

"What you grumping around about?" asked Uncle Henry.

"Not grumping," said Aunt Belle.

She stirred the onions and green peppers frying in the Dutch oven.

"Are too—been looking poop-faced for days now."

"Guess I'm a little worried about those two kids."

"Susan and Hank Jr.?"

"Hell no, they're fine—Jordan and Clara Belle."

"What's it with you and those two? Act like a brood sow protecting her piglets."

"Now, that's real nice, Henry. Calling me a pig, huh?"

She added ground beef to the mixture.

"Know what I mean, Hon? You do fret over'um like they were your own. Smells good, what you making?"

"Chili."

"We get any this time? Always taking it off to the riff-raff at the Salvation Army."

"Somebody besides her mother needs to. God knows that jackass brother of mine sure won't."

"Well, you gotta admit she's a tad different."

"So am I and that never bothered you."

"Bothered me, hell, it's why I married you—well, that and wanting to get you in the sack. But you weren't ever that different."

"You know better than that—always been odd one out in the bunch."

She stirred some more.

"Anyway, Clara Belle starts school in two weeks. I'm afraid Dayton High School isn't ready for her and Jordan has no idea what he's in for—or maybe he does."

She reached for the chili powder.

"Put in plenty of that stuff—hotter the better." He paused, "I can't believe the school—"

She stopped stirring and turned around, waving her spoon at him.

"Dammit, that's exactly what I mean. Because she looks a little strange, everybody thinks she's retarded or something—kid's smart—Mary Faith's been working with her at home—already reads some of Jordan's *Dick and Jane* books—not the problem."

"What is?"

"Oh, go to your office. I need to think…and get your mitts out of my chili."

Uncle Henry gave her a swat on her behind.

"You think too much."

"Out!"

Aunt Belle finished putting together the chili and her plan.

~

Saturday came and her niece and nephew arrived, and as always, with high expectations. She knew they wouldn't be thrilled that she was taking their playtime to have a conference. Susan was old enough to be in on her plan.

Aunt Belle met them on the back porch before they could head off to the wash house.

"Susan, take Clara Belle upstairs and show her the new stuff in the trunk for dress-ups. There're some new earrings I threw in I think she'll like."

"What's everybody else g-gonna do?"

"Well," said Aunt Belle, "Hank Jr. has to help Uncle Henry up at the office."

"I do?" said Hank Jr.

72

"Don't ask, just get up there, he'll tell you."

"What about D-Doo-Dah?"

"I have something to tell him—then he can go help Uncle Henry too."

"What the hel…" said Hank Jr.

"Watch your language, bud—time to play later. Come on, Jordan, follow me."

They walked through the kitchen, living room and dining room to the parlor.

"Hey, that's my p-parlor," Clara Belle said as she and Susan started up the stairs.

"Mind if Jordan and I use it for a little while? Then it'll be your turn."

"That's all r-right then."

Jordan followed Aunt Belle into the parlor.

"Aunt Belle," said Jordan, "you never did this with me before."

"Never needed to till now. Sit!"

He sat in the red velvet chair in the corner.

"You know Clara Belle's startin' school next week."

"So?"

"Thought about how that might be for her—for you?"

"Not much."

"But some, maybe?"

Jordan squirmed in his chair.

"Maybe."

Aunt Belle waited.

Jordan looked out the window and said, "I think maybe she might get teased 'cause she's, well, 'cause she's Clara Belle."

"How 'bout you?"

"Me?"

He got up and started walking around the room.

"Jordan, sit down."

He sat down, looking at the floor.

"Look at me, Jordan."

She saw his eyes fill up.

"I'm all mixed up, Aunt Belle. I want to do what you said, but it gets harder and harder. I was so scared when we did the snipe trick and I thought something had happened to her and then I was all mad at her when the trick was on us. I'm tired of being the one who takes up for her all the time. I just wanted to be on the other side for a change. She drives me crazy. "

"Jordan, I know; it's OK—that's why we need to talk. Maybe I can help you out—give you some ideas."

"Like what?"

"For starters, you gotta know those kids at Dayton will take one look at Clara Belle and think there's something wrong with her brain, which we both know there isn't. She'll take care of letting them know otherwise."

"But what about?...well you know."

"The rest of her?"

"Uh-huh."

"Remember how you used to feel early on? Treat her the way you did back then—might teach the others how to treat her."

"Like the golden rule, sorta?"

"Sorta. And, Jordan, I know it's hard. She's doing the best she can just being herself—you do the best you can and be yourself."

Aunt Belle sat very still and waited.

"Can I go play now?"

"Git!"

Jordan left the room and Aunt Belle shook her head and sighed—one down and one to go.

"Susan, send Clara Belle down to the parlor."

Clara Belle came down the stairs, her braced leg clunking and a pair of dangly earrings jingling.

"Look at me, Aunt B-Belle, just like you."

"Beautiful, a true gypsy goddess."

74

"Aunt Belle, what d-does it mean, 'black sheep of the family?' "

"Where'd you hear that?"

"My d-daddy says you're one."

Aunt Belle sighed.

"What do you think it means?"

Clara Belle thought for a minute.

"Means maybe if I looked d-down in our field in spring at all the new white lambs and saw a b-black one, that'd be the one I'd want to t-take home."

"Close enough."

"What'd you say to D-Doo-Dah?"

"Between me and him, just like our talks."

"I got a joke."

"Shoot."

"I'm a little teapot, short and stout," she sang, "here is my handle." She put her left hand on her hip with the suitable teapot-like bend in her arm, "here is my—" At this point she looked at her other arm, placed it identically to the left and delivered the punch line.

"Oh, what the hell, I'm a sugar bowl. TA-DAH!"

Aunt Belle threw back her head and laughed.

"Good one. Where—?"

"Boy in c-choir—what next?"

Aunt Belle walked to her old pine desk, rolled back the slatted cover and sitting inside was the rusted tin box.

"Mining for treasure," she said as she picked up the box and carried it to her chair.

"B-But all I saw in the wash house was old yellow papers. Where's the treasure?"

"In the papers."

Clara Belle waited for Aunt Belle to unwrap something wonderful from the folded papers.

Instead, Aunt Belle unfolded several sheets of yellowed stationery with writing on them.

"Gonna read you somethin'."

"OK, I guess."

"It's a letter somebody wrote a long time ago about a little girl about your age."

Clara Belle peered into the tin box again, hoping.

"Dear Pearl," Aunt Belle began.

"Who's—"

Aunt Belle gave her a "don't interrupt" look.

"Dear Pearl, couldn't wait to tell you this one on our kleine clown—"

"Hey, that's—"

"You want to hear this or not?"

Clara Belle nodded.

"...She really pulled a good one this time. Ben and I had to go to Richmond for one of his State Farm meetings. We decided to leave the other children at home. We went by train and stayed in a downtown Richmond hotel. Our room was on the bottom floor. It had a large plate glass window that looked out onto the sidewalk and a wide windowsill. Over the window was a thick brocade drapery. Ben came in after his meeting and said it was time to go to dinner. He asked where kleine Belle was—"

"I know, I know. This is about you."

"How'd you know?"

Clara Belle grinned.

"Since you already know... My mother, now this was my real mother, not the Grandmother Miller you know, looked in all the usual places, behind the furniture, under the bed, in the bathtub and, my favorite, the closet. At home I always hid there to play with the animals I dragged in off the farm before my daddy made me take them back. Couldn't find me anywhere. Daddy started gettin' riled up 'cause he was ready to go eat. Mother saw a little bulge in the curtain. She waved her hand for Daddy to be quiet and come with her. They walked out to the street; there I was, standing in the window, dressed up in one of my mother's flannel night-gowns, Sunday hat and gloves, and a long string of pearls.

Just stood there like I was a store dummy, with a blank look on my face, staring into space, not moving a muscle. People were walking by pointing and laughing and I didn't move 'cause I was having so much fun. I saw my daddy grab my mother's hand and pull her back inside—I heard him say. 'Get Belle out that window, Vada Pearl, she should not be making a spectacle. It's not becoming, yet.'

"My mother looked at my daddy and said, 'Look at her Ben, she's not afraid of what anybody says. She's having a wonderful time pretending she's not a little farm girl. She must have seen the mannequins in the Miller & Rhoads windows this morning when we went shopping. Let her be herself—she has a gift—you can be proud she's your daughter.'

"But he wasn't. He yanked me out of that window and—"

"And he s-spanked you," Clara Belle said quietly.

Aunt Belle shook her head.

"Know why I told you that story?"

"Cause your d-daddy didn't like you, like mine."

"Clara Belle, your daddy loves you and my daddy… well, they just have a little trouble understanding us. We're a special kind, you and I. We like to dress our way, talk our way and be funny just like God made us to be."

"G-God thinks I'm funny?"

"You bet He does."

"Even the b-bunny fart joke?"

"Especially that one."

"Now one more thing. School."

"I'm going to Dayton like D-Doo-Dah."

"Listen real careful."

She cleared her throat and took a deep breath.

"There might be some kids there, and even some teachers maybe, who'll be like your daddy and my daddy and won't understand. What's important is to always be who you are."

"Doo-Dah d-doesn't think I'm as funny much anymore."

"Jordan might be a big help—let him."

Aunt Belle shook her head and pulled Clara Belle close to her. She wasn't much of a hugger, but she knew when somebody needed one. She gave her niece a quick squeeze and whispered, "Now, let's say it together, one more time."

The two of them held hands and repeated the secret and sacred words together. Clara Belle asked the question—Aunt Belle gave the answer.

"Good girl," said Aunt Belle.

"But where's the tr—"

"Time to go play now," said Aunt Belle, and the session in the parlor was over.

Chapter 12

THE DIFFERENT KIND OF LAUGHING

He really was going to try today, but he was scared he might foul up. He and Clara Belle had talked a little about the first day of school, but not much. She had acted kind of funny after that Saturday at Aunt Belle's, like she was waiting for him to say or do something.

"Clara Belle, I've got an idea for the bus this morning," he said when Aunt Mary Faith brought her over to his house to walk down the lane.

"What idea?"

"Well, this will be your first time on the bus and since nobody's ever seen you before, maybe we need a plan."

"A plan f-for what?"

"To help the kids understand about you."

She didn't argue, and he was surprised when she seemed to know exactly what he was talking about.

"Here's what we'll do. When the bus comes and we get on, I'll go first."

Clara Belle was quiet and waited.

"Then I'll help you up the steps and say, This is Clara Belle Miller and she's my cousin. Then you tell the bunny-fart joke, and everybody will like you right off. How 'bout that?"

"That's great, D-Doo-Dah. Do you think it'll work?"

"Sure it will," he said, crossing his fingers. "Let's get going. We don't want to be late your first day."

Aunt Mary Faith had been talking to his mother. When she got ready to leave, she said, "Hey, you two, why don't I walk with you down to the bus."

"I d-don't want to be treated like a baby. I can walk with Doo-Dah by myself."

"All right then," Aunt Mary Faith said. "How about I walk halfway down the lane and wait until you get on the bus?"

"Don't you d-dare yell goodbye or wave or anything. Promise?" Clara Belle commanded.

"Promise," agreed Aunt Mary Faith.

They walked down the lane, and just as Aunt Mary Faith had promised, she stopped halfway, sat down under a tree and watched until she saw the bus—she didn't wave or yell goodbye.

"You ready?" said Jordan.

"I was b-born ready."

Jordan got on the bus first and looked down the long rows of seats where there were a few kids from church, but most of them had never seen Clara Belle. He turned to the bus driver.

"Mr. Howdyshell, I need to help my cousin on the bus. She has a brace."

"Sure, Jordan, take your time. Good morning, young lady. First day of school?"

Clara Belle nodded her head as Jordan held her hand and pulled her up to the front of the bus.

"Find a seat; we're already a little late," said Mr. Howdyshell.

"But we need to do something."

"Sorry, kids, no time. Take your seat."

Jordan spotted two seats near the back and said, "Come on, Clara Belle, we can sit back there." As they walked to the back of the bus, everybody stopped talking and Clara Belle's brace kept bumping against the seats. Even the kids who knew them from church didn't say hello or anything.

As soon as they were settled in their seats, the whispers started.

"What's that?"

"Look at her hair."

"What's that on her leg?"

"What's wrong with her eyes?"

"T-Tell it now?" Clara Belle said, trying to whisper. Everybody turned around at the sound of her voice.

Jordan shook his head, "I don't think so, not now, nobody could hear it with the bus running—maybe later. Just don't talk until we get there."

Usually when Jordan flat out told Clara Belle what to do, she told him to "go to hell" and did exactly what she pleased. Today, for some reason, she did what he said.

The short ride down Route 42 to the little town of Dayton seemed like forever. They made two more stops, turned right at the big gray cannon on Hill Street and went up the street to Dayton High School. Everything looked the same but he knew that this year things might be a little different.

The bus pulled to the back of the building where the students got out. There was a line of busses so they had to wait.

"Now, Doo-Dah?"

It was now or never.

"OK, here goes."

He looked around for somebody from Sunday school.

"Billy, you know my cousin Clara Belle—she's funny isn't she?" he said loudly.

"Well, yeah, she's pretty funny at choir."

This got everyone's attention.

"Everybody, this is my cousin Clara Belle and she has a good riddle."

All eyes were on Clara Belle.

"Knock, knock."

Jordan wasn't ready. Where was the bunny-fart joke?

"Knock, knock," she said again.

"Who's there?"

"Cowsgo."

"Cowsgo, who?"

"No they don't—they go moo."

Some of the kids laughed a little.

Someone said, "I already heard that one."

Someone else said, "That's dumb."

The bus driver opened the door and said, "OK, kids, out you go."

"Let's wait till everybody else gets off," Jordan whispered.

"I want to g-go in now," Clara Belle said.

Since Clara Belle was sitting on the aisle, Jordan couldn't stop her. She stood up and pushed herself to the front of the bus.

"Excuse me—p-pardon me—sorry—excuse me."

He finally caught up with her and helped her off the bus. He tried not to look at anybody as he took her to the first grade classroom where Miss Cline stood waiting at the door.

"Good morning, Clara Belle, we're glad to have you," Miss Cline said with a look that gave Jordan the feeling maybe she wasn't. She took Clara Belle's hand and led her into the room. Jordan made a quick getaway.

Jordan was happy to see his classmates he hadn't seen all summer. He took his seat beside Danny Holsinger who had been on the bus. Danny looked at Jordan, whispered something to Bobby Showalter, and they both laughed. He started to bite his fingernails—by the time the lunch bell rang they were down to a nub.

Everybody at Dayton High ate in the same cafeteria downstairs in the basement of the school. They ate in shifts—elementary school kids first, then the high school. The first and second graders went in together and, when they were finishing up, the third and fourth graders started through the line. Most of the kids who lived on farms, like Jordan, brought lunches from home, but he usually bought a one dollar, five-day lunch ticket for one simple reason—the food those ladies fixed in that stainless steel kitchen was delicious. What they could do with a grilled cheese sandwich and tomato soup was gourmet. Fat slices of yellow farm cheese were put between two pieces of white Sunbeam bread. The bread was brushed with real butter on the outside, then grilled until the sandwich was crisp and brown and the cheese inside was melted, hot and gooey.

The smell of today's lunch crept its way up the two staircases into his classroom, and by the time his class was scheduled to eat, Jordan was starved—he was sure he smelled grilled cheese.

Jordan's class was lined up outside the cafeteria door, waiting to get their lunch tickets punched. The first and second-graders were almost finished and he craned his neck to see if he could find Clara Belle. His heart sank when he saw her eating all alone beside Miss Cline at a table next to the door to the playground. She was putting back her thermos in her Roy Rogers lunch box when she spotted him. A broad grin came across her face and she yelled out across the cafeteria in her loudest voice, "Doo-Dah, hey!" Again she shouted, "Hey, D-Doo-Dah, it's me."

Jordan's face turned red and he edged behind a supporting post, trying to disappear, but he could feel the stares of everyone in the cafeteria. He managed a weak wave to Clara Belle, along with a hard look that would signal to her that she needed to shut up immediately—she didn't. Instead she shouted across a very quiet cafeteria.

"Hey, Doo-Dah, what's invisible and—"

"Not here, Clara Belle, not now," Jordan said quickly.

Jordan was almost relieved when Buddy Shifflet yelled, "Hey, Doo-Dah, hey, Doo-Dah."

At first, there were only a few giggles, but soon everybody in the cafeteria was laughing. They looked from Jordan to Clara Belle, then back to Jordan. He waited and finally drummed up enough courage to look her way—Clara Belle was laughing, too. Jordan knew she didn't understand that this was a different kind of laughing. As the teachers tried to calm everybody down, Jordan heard Buddy Shifflet's voice again, "Yeah, D-Doo-Dah and the d-d-dummy. Stupidity must run in the family."

Jordan grabbed his arm and pulled him to the linoleum floor, yelling, "You take that back, you hear. Take it back!" They bumped into one of the long tables and a first grader's thermos crashed to the floor, spilling chocolate milk all over both of them. The girls were screaming, the boys were cheering them on, and the teachers were blowing their recess whistles when Mr. Mills, the principal, came in and pulled Buddy and Jordan apart, lifted them up by the backs of their shirts and dragged them out of the cafeteria. Jordan looked over his shoulder to see where Clara Belle had gone. She had made her escape out the side door of the cafeteria and was sitting in a swing on the playground.

Mr. Mills took them in his office and gave them "down the country" about fighting, something Jordan had never done his entire life until that day—then he called their parents. Jordan had never been in Mr. Mills' office except for times when he carried notes from the teacher, a job that only responsible students were asked to do. His mother came to pick him up and she was not happy. The ride home was quiet and uncomfortable. When they got in the house his mother asked, "All right, young man, just exactly what happened today at school?"

"Oh, you know what a bully Buddy is; he just pushed me too far, no big deal—I promise it won't ever happen again."

But Jordan knew deep inside that the lie he had told was much bigger than he was letting on. Suddenly he thought of Clara Belle coming home on the bus by herself.

"Mom, please, let me go meet Clara Belle at the end of the lane. She might need some help."

"You can go to meet her, but come straight home. And for the next week you can't go anywhere after school."

Jordan ran down the lane and waited nervously at the bus stop.

The big yellow bus slowed to a stop. The door opened. He saw her walk very carefully down the steps—the bus driver handed her her book bag—they were laughing. A good sign, Jordan thought. But when he got closer, he saw the dried streaks of tears wiped with a dirty hand. As she came close, he looked into her eyes for the signal that would tell him what was going on inside her and what he saw scared him a little. There was no twinkle, but there was a light—a new kind of light—more like a tiny fire.

"Tomorrow will be better," she said.

Chapter 13

THE DIFFERENT KIND OF CLOWN

"Tomorrow will be better," Clara Belle had predicted that September afternoon at the end of the lane, and this proved to be true—at least to a degree. From that day, she never called him "Doo-Dah" outside the family and their private world.

Of course, this didn't solve nearly everything because Clara Belle was, after all, Clara Belle. Jordan had expected her to seem a little different but she stuck out like a sore thumb. Since the morning he had first seen her, he had accepted Clara Belle exactly as she was—now he wanted her to change, to fit in.

"Can't'cha just talk a little softer, Clara Belle?" he suggested. "Maybe you wouldn't bother the other kids as much."

"Why would I d-do that?" she roared. "Nobody would pay any attention to me."

He made other suggestions, which met with the same resistance.

"I won't change b-because of anyone else but me."

Granddaddy Miller had named her "kleine clown," Pennsylvania Dutch for little clown. She had lived up to the name and brought home riddles and jokes she had heard in school, adapting them to her unique performance style for the cousins at family gatherings.

Clara Belle must have decided that this act of hers, fairly successful at home and at Sunday school, would also work at school. What Jordan saw at school was different. The first time he saw this new clown in action he barely recognized the kleine clown.

Clara Belle and Jordan's recesses were scheduled at the same time but on different sections of the playground. He seldom even caught a glimpse of Clara Belle. The younger kids played at the bottom of the hill where there was a small swing set, several seesaws and a little merry-go-round. On the upper level were larger swings and the best piece of playground equipment ever invented—it was called "The Wave." The thing had a large steel pole in the center. From the top of the center pole, smaller steel rods, like supports for an Indian teepee, reached downward and were connected to a wooden bench circling the pole. The Wave swung both from side to side, around in a circle and as the name suggested, in waves, up, down and around.

One day Jordan's class was coming out for recess when he noticed Clara Belle down at the lower level talking to a little girl. Aunt Mary and Clara Belle still fought about her clothes but she usually wore her balloon pants. None of the other girls ever wore pants to school, only a dress or skirt.

The other little girl was teasing Clara Belle, "Why're you wearin' those stupid pants? You look like a dumb clown." Jordan moved closer so he could hear what was going on.

Clara Belle thought a minute and said, "Of course I d-do; I have an aunt who was a clown in the circus and these used to b-be hers. She taught me some tricks. Watch this."

She began running, limping along, and attempted a cartwheel. She almost managed the trick, but when she landed on the leg with the brace, it gave way and she rolled, pell mell on the grass, stopping just short of the sidewalk. She didn't move and Jordan could see by the look on her face that she was hurt. Before he could go down to her, she suddenly leaped up, raised both hands in the air as she always did for the finale of her jokes, smiled a big smile and bellowed in that outrageous voice, "Ta-Dah!" The other little girl burst into giggles and applause and that was the debut of Clara Belle the Clown Show at school. This was also when she started telling semi-lies. Her tale hadn't been a total lie since

Aunt Belle had once hidden in a tent after the circus shut down for the night because she wanted to join the clowns. Her ploy hadn't worked because Granddaddy Miller had missed her about milking time and went to the fairgrounds with the Irish wolfhound, which sniffed her out. At school that day Jordan decided that if Clara Belle were going to tell at least part of the truth, he wouldn't snitch on her if the strategy helped her make friends more easily.

Chapter 14

THE PARLOR TALK, TOO

"Aunt Belle, I need to talk to you about somethin'," said Jordan. "It's about Clara Belle."

Jordan's father had come to talk business with Uncle Henry, and Jordan could, for once, have a conversation with Aunt Belle without Clara Belle's presence. They went into the kitchen.

"Whassup, buddy?"

"Well, I don't exactly know how to start. It's kinda hard to say."

"Best way to start is by startin' with the truth, Jordan. Can't say anything would surprise or upset me and it won't ever go any farther than the front of my face."

"Well, like I said, it's about Clara Belle—me and her at school. You know how I always take up for her and stuff, and I like her and all, but to tell the honest truth, Aunt Belle, she's turning into somebody I don't even know anymore."

"Give me a for instance," said Aunt Belle.

"OK, you know how funny she is with us and we all laugh with her—except Uncle Ben, maybe? At school she goes overboard just to be funny. I guess she's trying to fit with the ones who laugh behind her back, but they're laughin' at her, not with her. They think she's a freak, not like we think she's a kleine clown."

"Talked to Clara Belle 'bout this?"

"Uh, well, no, I don't see her that much anymore—fourth graders aren't with first graders, you know."

"Ever try?"

There was a huge silence as Jordan pondered the question he had been asking himself for months. He couldn't speak the truth, even to Aunt Belle, because the truth was that for the first time since Clara Belle had come into his life she embarrassed him.

As if reading his mind, just like Clara Belle, Aunt Belle said, "Jordan, you're a great cousin to Clara Belle—helped her since the first day you saw her. Wasn't hard then—now you're embarrassed. Nothin' too strange about that at your age.

"I understand and maybe Clara Belle does, too. We have our little parlor talks and discuss things like that—she knows you love her."

"Sometimes I don't act like I do. I pretend I don't see her when I really do and stuff like that. I get mad at myself, but I can't help it."

"Anything she does at school you can be proud of?"

"Well, yeah, I guess so. She's the smartest one in her class—never plays dumb even if the other kids'd prob'ly like her better if she did. Nobody like her ever went to Dayton High. She looks different and acts different, so kids and the teachers expect her to be stupid. It drives the other kids nuts when someone they think is not right in the head asks better questions than they do and makes better grades. Even if I am proud of her for that, it just makes things worse for her and she starts actin' even goofier."

Jordan hesitated, took a deep breath and posed the all-important question. "Aunt Belle, what about my being cho—?"

"Do the best ya can, buddy," Aunt Belle said and Jordan knew that their discussion was over.

The school year ended in June, and as Jordan and Clara Belle walked up the lane on the last day, Clara Belle threw her books on the ground, looked up to the sky and with her arms extended wide, she spun around in a circle three times yelling, "Ta-Dah, now I'm free, now I'm free!" On her face was an expression Jordan hadn't seen for a long time. The Kleine Clown was back.

Chapter 15

THE PROPHET SPEAKS, TOO

~Melinda~

I think my Aunt Dorcas really believed in her heart that Episcopalians were, at best, misguided, at worst, doomed and having little chance of being redeemed. That's why she had taken me to the Christmas pageant at Garber's Church and that's why she insisted that I go to Vacation Bible School. Although this was a nondenominational Bible school, I'm quite sure Aunt Dorcas would not have included my church as a denomination at all. Bible school was held at Dayton High School the end of July, about the time parents were ready to get their kids away from the freewheeling summer schedule into something structured—especially something structured by somebody else.

Classes were divided according to age, but since I went to elementary school in the city of Harrisonburg, I knew absolutely no one. I did, however, recognize a face—the face of Joseph, the father of the baby Jesus—from the Christmas pageant. I learned that his name was Jordan Glick and that he was from the clan of Millers who lived on Miller's Barn Farm between Harrisonburg and Dayton. Like most of the boys his age, he had little interest in religious studies, but unlike them, he did not try to disrupt the class. He was rather quiet and spent most of his time doodling on his workbook. I thought he was cute—he ignored me.

Most of the material was middle of the road religious education: learning Bible verses, discussions of what the teachings of the Bible said about how to treat other people—nothing controversial or even thought provoking.

His name was Brother Sam Garber and he was a missionary in China. He had been asked by Aunt Dorcas to speak to us at an assembly in the gym.

"Now boys and girls," Brother Garber began, "I am a missionary in China. I am there to bring the Word of God to them. The Chinese and other heathen people like them all over the world live in great darkness and their lives are in peril. If they don't confess that Jesus is God's only Son, they can never go to heaven and will be doomed to an eternity in hell with the Devil himself. It is the only way a heathen can be saved."

I saw a small arm raise in the front row where the second graders sat.

"Yes, child?"

"Excuse me, Brother Garber, but aren't we all God's children? Doesn't God love everybody?" said a familiar voice.

Where had I heard that voice before?

Brother Garber cleared his throat loudly and said, "Please stand up, little one, what is your name?"

"Clara Belle Miller, sir," said the throaty voice I now remembered from the Christmas pageant. She stood and all I could see from my seat was that pink-red, frizzy hair. She hadn't grown an inch since I saw her almost two years ago.

"Well, Clara Belle Miller," continued Brother Garber, not hiding his irritation at this questioning of his authority, "of course we are all God's children, but if the heathen people of China are not truly saved, then their souls are lost to Him."

"But what if they are good people and love each other and treat each other with kindness like Jesus tells us to do?"

There was a titter of voices and giggles around me and the boy named Jordan turned beet red and covered his face with his hands.

Brother Garber frowned and coughed before he managed a weak and very fake smile.

"They still have to speak the words that Jesus is their personal savior."

"But—"

"If there are no more questions, let us pray."

~

Friday, the last day of Bible school, we all gathered for a picnic on the lawn in front of the school. I still hadn't made any headway with Jordan who seemed even more remote after the incident in the gym.

I looked up at the school building and on the tiered steps was a bunch of children.

They were sitting in two rows, looking like a miniature church congregation. Standing in front was Clara Belle Miller. She looked like she was giving a sermon and her congregation was hanging onto her every word. She still had that booming voice and she was really excited about what she was saying.

"Poor Brother Sam, the missionary man, he just doesn't understand the Chinese at all. I bet he never even read about Confucius, Lao-tse, and Buddha and what they told the Chinese people about how to live a good life."

I moved close enough to hear, which didn't have to be that close.

"To begin with, there were three main preachers in China and the first one was Confucius. He lived a long time ago and told the Chinese people to be honest and not to lie and cheat. He said they should obey their mothers and daddies, grandmothers and granddaddies and their aunts and uncles and be nice and listen to their friends." She emphasized the last group and gave them a stern look, making sure they were listening to her.

"Most important, he said that they must not do to others anything that they wouldn't want done to them, which sounds real familiar in a back-ass-wards sort of way, don't you think?"

The children looked at each other, obviously shocked at her language, but intrigued enough to look back at their speaker, wanting to hear more.

"You mean like the Golden Rule?" one boy asked.

"Exactly, good for you," she said.

"He also said that if you fill your head with nice and lovely thoughts as much as possible, the world would be a better place. All of his sayings were written down on rocks in a monastery by monks who read them all the time and shaved their heads.

"Confucius lived longer than Moses and then he died. Then along came a guy named Lao-tse and he told the Chinese almost the same thing, but added some more stuff to it, like when people died, they would come back to life again. So, if that was true, you ought to live your life sharing and being good to people and taking care of nature because if you messed up the earth, when you came back there wouldn't be a decent place to live. He used fancy language and sayings, too, but I don't think they wrote his on rocks. I think he used pencil and paper."

Even in my liberal Episcopal upbringing, I hadn't been exposed to any of this information. Where would a seven-year-old Brethren kid get it? The children were getting fidgety—I was mesmerized.

"This is the last guy, then I'm finished," she said, realizing she might be losing her audience.

"The last preacher to come along was Buddha, only he wasn't called Buddha to start out with—he was a rich prince with a wife and kids. When he got fired up, he just up and left and wandered around, trying to find the answer to life. That doesn't seem quite right to me to leave your wife and kids in the lurch, but he did it anyway. He believed what Confucius and Lao-tse said was almost right but had to add his two-cents worth. He said that you should help people that needed it right now and he called heaven Nirvana, which was like living on a really perfect earth. He said we should pay attention to 'now', not yesterday or tomorrow—now. After he figured this all out, he went around preaching all over China. Then he got old and bald and fat and the Chinese started making statues of him with his belly button sticking out because they believed what he said was important.

"It seems to me—" Aunt Dorcas had just come down from the office and was listening to Clara Belle wind up her sermon.

"It seems to me that Jesus would have agreed with most everything these three preachers said. In fact, he said most of the very same things but in a different way. Maybe if Brother Sam, the missionary man, would take time to listen a little more to what the Chinese people really believed in their hearts, he might want to spend more time feeding the ones who are starving and giving medicine to the ones who are sick, the way Jesus said to do, instead of trying to scare the hell out of them. Amen."

Clara Belle's face had that same look she'd had at the Christmas pageant. She was radiant standing there, waiting for applause, cheers—anything.

There was nothing save a great silence as little mouths dropped open and big eyes looked over to my aunt to see what would happen next. Aunt Dorcas couldn't speak for a moment and I could see she was searching for the right words.

Clara Belle looked at Aunt Dorcas. Her face fell from a height of pure prophetic zeal to the depths of a stark reality.

In a very calm and icy voice, Aunt Dorcas said, "Children, you mustn't pay any mind to what Clara Belle has just said. She's been misled and is completely wrong in her thinking. Brother Garber has told you the truth. Now, go gather your things; it's time to go home."

"Clara Belle, I will talk with your parents about where you have gotten this information and I am quite sure they'll make certain you never are exposed to it again. This behavior is not becoming, Clara Belle, of a good Christian girl. Now go to the bus immediately."

Aunt Dorcas looked toward me and continued in her steely monotone, "Melinda, please go to my car."

Clara Belle's whole body seemed to cave in on itself. Her limp, which had almost disappeared as she paced back and forth during her oration, was now pronounced as she walked past me. She glanced my way, and everything in me wanted to say, "I loved what you said,"—but I didn't.

Chapter 16

THE FAIR TO MIDDLIN'

Although the situation with Clara Belle had been somewhat easier for Jordan during that summer after her second grade year, the difference in their ages was beginning to take a toll on their close relationship. Incidents like the Bible school "sermon" embarrassed and alienated Jordan more and more. Even activities they had always enjoyed together like the public pool in Harrisonburg or going to Saturday matinees were strained when he was forced to choose between his friends and his cousin.

At the end of August, just as the fall air began to sneak up on mornings and evenings, it was fair time. The Rockingham County Fair was a major event in the area, not only for farm folk, but also for everyone around. Unlike county fairs in many parts of the country, this one was "clean," meaning there was no midway with crooked games or sleazy shows—Jordan and Clara Belle's Uncle John made certain of that. He had been president of the fair committee since its beginnings and felt personally responsible for keeping "his fair" a safe place for young people to hang out, even at night. There were only three rides: the Ferris wheel, the swings and the merry-go-round, but that was plenty and even the best cooks in the county waited in line for the French fries, hamburgers and deep-fried chicken from the Ruritan food booth. Games of chance were not rigged, which assured that Jordan could win Clara Belle a stuffed animal by throwing balls into a pyramid of wooden bottles.

This year's fair presented a problem for Jordan. In years past, he and Clara Belle had always gone to the fair together, enjoying the wonders of the rides, midway, shows, and buildings full of fascinating commercial exhibits from the Culligan Soft Water Man to the newest Singer Sewing Machine. What Aunt Belle had warned him about was coming true—he didn't like being around her when his friends were around. He'd tried but, except with family where he acted like always, he pretty much stayed away from her—sometimes he felt real bad about it, too.

"D-Doo-Dah, when are we going to the fair?" asked Clara Belle as she sat in the loft of the barn, watching him groom his sheep.

"Not sure, Clara Belle—ya know I'm gonna have to spend a lot of time with my sheep before the judgin' day after tomorrow and, well, you might just have to find somebody else to hang around with."

"Let me remind you, you sheep t-turd, that Uncle John only lets us in f-free if we're together. He won't even know who you are unless I'm with you."

Jordan knew she was right, of course. Uncle John, for some reason, never recognized him as kin and that was essential when it came to getting in both the entrance gate and shows. But he just had to break free from Clara Belle. His image among fellow members of the Dayton 4-H Club was at stake. He would be showing his first project at the fair this year and he couldn't have his nutty cousin hanging around the barns with his friends.

Being a member of the 4-H Club was something Jordan had looked forward to for years. All of the Millers had distinguished themselves as All-Stars in the organization, and when Jordan said the 4-H pledge at each meeting, "I pledge my head to clearer thinking, my heart to greater loyalty, my hands to larger service, my health to better living; for my club, my community and my country: To make the Best, Better," he just felt better about himself.

He most definitely needed some "clearer thinking" right now to devise a plan that would reap the benefits of Uncle John's position, using Clara Belle, yet would not jeopardize his freedom to be alone with his fellow 4-H buddies.

"These kids are with the show," said Uncle John as Jordan and Clara Belle walked by the man at the ticket gate the first day of the fair without paying a dime. They got on the Ferris wheel and knew that they would get an extra five rounds. Later, when Uncle John bought them a hamburger at the Ruritan stand, the women threw in a free order of fries. Jordan had decided that these benefits were worth the sacrifice of a little extra time with his cousin—but only this first day. Tomorrow would be another story.

That evening on the way home he laid the groundwork.

"I'll be getting my sheep ready all morning for the judgin'. Nobody but people involved with the livestock are allowed around the barns."

"You mean I can't come d-down at all?"

"You can watch the judgin' just like everybody else, but you can't talk to me at all—it's against the rules." This was an outright lie and he knew he wasn't near as good at it as Clara Belle.

"They'll deduct points if I'm distracted durin' the judgin' so you stay far away so I won't even know you're there. This is real important and I have a good chance to win a blue ribbon. If I win, I'll treat you to somethin' neat with my prize money."

He knew that was the clincher. Clara Belle bought his lie, hook, line and sinker and stayed as far away from him as possible all that day.

At the end of the day, his sheep came in fourth in a field of four. He would get no cash prize, only a ribbon. There would be no "something neat" for Clara Belle and when Uncle John told her that her cousin had been lying all the time, she was so furious that she ignored him the rest of the fair. She continued on alone, getting in free for shows, free rides and free fries, and even though Jordan missed the perks, he got his way, spending the entire fair week down at the barns with his friends.

The last day, guilt and a powerful hunger for free food and fun finally got to Jordan.

"Clara Belle, we haven't spent much time together this week—why don't we hang around together tonight? We'll go to the horse show for a while and watch the fireworks in the back of the pickup."

"OK, I guess so, but you missed all the b-best stuff already; the pet show was Thursday and the g-gospel quartet was last night. You really are a shit you know, lying like you d-did, but I forgive you because you are my favorite c-cousin and you need me desperately. Come on, Doo-Dah, let's have some fun."

And they did. They rode every ride for free, ate extra fries at the Ruritan booth and he won Clara Belle a stuffed clown with red hair at the penny-throw. As they walked to the pickup truck to watch the fireworks, Jordan glanced at his cousin, clutching the image of herself in her arms, and felt an unexpected catch in his throat.

Chapter 17

THE SONG OF THE SOUTH

"Hey, D-Doo-Dah, you want to go to the Saturday matinee this week? I've only got a little more t-time to, well, you know."

And Jordan did know. Once again his cousin would have to struggle to fit in at school and temper her behavior—not an easy task. His task, that of keeping his distance, would be easier. As a fifth grader, he would be physically apart most of the day and never have lunch or recess with her second grade class. So, even though he was wary after the Bible school performance, he said, "Sure, Clara Belle, just this one last time."

Clara Belle gave him a puzzled look, then shrugged her shoulders and sighed.

For Clara Belle, the movies at the Saturday matinee provided a balance to her weekday struggles to survive in the "real world." There in the dark, she whiled away Saturday mornings absorbed in a universe of fantasy, buttered popcorn and Pepsi. In the world of the movies there was an orchestra playing in the background, beautiful women and handsome men burst into song in the middle of the forest or walking down the street in the rain. Happy endings were mandatory, large choruses of women danced up and down stairs in beautiful costumes, and Esther Williams could swim underwater forever, without taking a breath or closing her eyes, and she always smiled.

Aunt Belle picked up the two of them after breakfast, drove the short distance to Harrisonburg and dropped them off at the Virginia Theater on Main Street. There they had sat many times for three hours of cartoons, coming attractions,

Movietone News, a serial movie and a main feature. This weekly ritual had always been pure joy, pure make-believe.

The feature movie that day was a Walt Disney production called *Song of the South*. Uncle Remus, a slave, told wonderful stories to Johnny and Ginny, the young boy and girl who lived on the plantation. His yarns about Brer Rabbit, Brer Fox and Brer Bear were filled with folksy wisdom and the children were held spellbound for hours to the dismay of the adults in the film. Uncle Remus, Johnny and Ginny were live actors, while the stories he told were illustrated by cartoons.

When Uncle Remus came skipping down the road, surrounded by all those animated birds and bunnies, singing the "Zip-A-Dee-Doo-Dah" song, Clara Belle went berserk.

"Did you hear that, he j-just sang your name! Can you believe it? Zip-A-Dee-Doo-Dah, Doo-Dah, for P-Pete's sake!" she yelled. A girl in front of them turned around and stared at Clara Belle incredulously.

"What are you looking at?" said Clara Belle, who couldn't have whispered if she tried. "Turn b-back around and watch the movie."

The girl did.

Hoping to calm her down before the usher appeared, Jordan feigned excitement and said, "Yeah, Clara Belle, that's real cool," which seemed to satisfy her for the moment.

The story continued and Clara Belle never said another word throughout the entire movie.

When they came out of the theater she was unusually quiet and Jordan knew the signs—she was in the process of having serious thoughts. As soon as they got into Aunt Belle's car she asked Aunt Belle, "Aunt B-Belle, were there really slaves?"

"Yep—long time ago—not anymore."

"Were they all Negroes?"

"Yep."

"Why?"

"Don't know, Clara Belle. Just the way it was."

"Did the white p-people really own the slaves like a horse or a cow?"

"Guess you might say that."

"They didn't get p-paid anything to work?"

"Nope, master gave them a place to live and food to eat."

"D-did they have anything that was their own?"

"Don't think so."

She waited a long time before she said, "That movie wasn't really true. Uncle Remus s-smiled and acted happy all the time. What d-did he have to be happy about?"

The question seemed to stump even Aunt Belle and she didn't answer. The car was quiet for a full five minutes while Clara Belle waited for Aunt Belle's usual words of wisdom—they never came.

Finally, Aunt Belle broke the silence. "You kids wanna go to Kline's for a frozen custard?" Both of them yelled, "Yeah," and they were off to North Main to get a sugar cone, Uncle Remus forgotten.

~ Melinda~

"I really don't think Melinda should see so many movies," said my Aunt Dorcas to my mother. "They are a bad influence on a young mind."

As sisters, they couldn't have been more different when it came to religion. My mother had married an Episcopalian and felt that she had thankfully escaped some of the more narrow views of her upbringing. Aunt Dorcas had never married and became wed to her own distorted interpretation of an already conservative denomination.

"For Pete's sake, Dorcas, it's a Disney film. How influential could it be? It's just a piece of fluff, " said my mother.

"But, she's already—"

"It's really good," I said. "I want to see it again. I like how the cartoons and real people are on the screen at the same time. It's just a fun movie, not serious or anything."

I was waiting in the lobby of the theater and there she was again—the girl named Clara Belle. I knew she had been there last Saturday because I had sat right in front of her. When she had started making such a scene about the "Zip-A-Dee-Doo-Dah" song I looked around and saw her and Jordan, who was trying to shut her up. When she told me to turn around and watch the movie, I did.

I'm sure she hadn't remembered me from Bible school but I remembered her and waited to see just what she might be up to.

Today she was standing by one of the two entrances to the balcony, looking up at a sign posted above the door. I saw Jordan cross the lobby toward her and when she spotted him, she said, "Do you know what that sign means?" She pointed to the one above her head, which said "White Balcony."

Most likely that sign had been there for years—I had never noticed it.

"That means," she continued, "that you and I can go to the white balcony but a Negro can't—he has to go to that balcony over there." She pointed her finger to the other side of the lobby where, over the door, there hung a sign saying "Colored Balcony."

Her voice bounced off the walls and high ceiling of the theater lobby as if amplified. As other children arrived, she began to draw an audience, which was obviously what she had in mind.

"Did you know," she said, planting herself nose to nose with a little blond boy about five, "it's been eighty-five years since Negroes were set free from being slaves? If they're free, why can't they go to any balcony they want?"

The boy stood frozen as Clara Belle glared at him with her blue eyes blazing, her red hair frizzing and her unanswered question poised like a snake ready to strike. "Mommy, Mommy, help me," he screamed, finally breaking her gaze and running the other way. "That girl is crazy."

"Clara Belle," Jordan pleaded, "you scared the daylights out of that kid. Why don't we go in the theater? Since it's so early we could get a good seat."

"Go on in, I've got work to do," she said as she looked around, singling out her next target.

I watched with fascination and shock as she marched over to a Negro girl of about ten.

"And it's just not fair that you can't go to a regular school, or ride in the front of a bus or even drink at that water fountain over there," she said pointing to the sign that said "Whites Only."

The girl's jaw dropped and her chocolate brown eyes seemed to grow larger than her face. She watched with astonishment as the strange creature with hair as nappy as her own, only pink, walked across the lobby.

"You see that Negro boy over there?" she asked the gathering crowd. "He can't drink out of our water fountain, but you just watch. Nobody would say a word if I do this."

I, along with a lobby full of brown and white children, watched as she walked over to the water fountain where there was another sign saying, "Colored Only." She stopped in front of the water fountain and announced in her booming voice, "Boy, I sure am thirsty."

Not altogether positive she had the undivided attention of every person in the lobby, she said again, even louder, "Boy, I sure am thirsty."

Convinced that the time was right, she turned her back to her audience, stood on her tiptoes to reach the spout, then turned on the water fountain, took a big swallow, wiped her mouth and said with a self-satisfied grin on her face, "That sure was good."

There wasn't a sound in the lobby except the popping of corn as she stretched her tiny body as tall as it would go, and with her wild red hair flying, her head held high, she moved toward the stairs to the Colored Balcony.

"And this movie isn't true. Uncle Remus was a slave. He couldn't have been *that* happy."

She disappeared up the stairs.

Nobody knew what to do next. Even the popcorn popper was silent. An usher finally gained his composure and said to the crowd, "All right folks, let's move on into the theater, the movie's about to start." Relieved to have some reasonable directions, the children began to file into their appropriate areas as the usher went up the stairs to retrieve Clara Belle.

Jordan ducked into the theater downstairs.

I couldn't enjoy the movie that day. Everything was different—something had changed.

Chapter 18

THE TRUTH AND SOME CONSEQUENCES

"Yes, Ben Jr.," Aunt Belle said into the phone, "I heard—they really tell her she couldn't come back?

"Well, yes, she probably got most of it from me. She—

"We got some books from the library and talked about it in the parlor this week.

"If you feel that way—" and she hung up.

"What a solid gold shit." She picked up a plate and threw it across the room. The plate didn't break—it was plastic, which made her even madder.

"Dammit to hell." She picked up the plate again but before she could throw it, Uncle Henry came into the kitchen and gently took it out of her hand.

"What in the world, woman?"

"Clara Belle pulled one of her stunts, and I think she's gone too far this time."

"You mean defending the nig—"

She slapped him across the face. She'd never done that—ever.

"Oh, God, Henry, I'm sorry, you know how I hate that word."

He rubbed his cheek and glared at her.

She wasn't sure what to do next. "I won't ev—"

He turned and walked out of the kitchen.

She'd gone too far. The one person who might understand and she'd hauled off and hit him. Better go out and make up—no, he'd cool off—deal with him later. What about Clara Belle? Who else could she talk to?

"Jordan," she said as she dialed the Glicks.

"Kate—Belle—Jordan there?…Thanks."

She waited.

"Busy, he's too…Homework?…*Sure* he is. Never mind…" She hung up.

She'd seen this coming. Clara Belle's behavior was driving Jordan farther and farther away—from both of them. Couldn't blame the kid—a teenager—a younger cousin like Clara Belle was a social nightmare.

She saw Uncle Henry smoking a cigarette out in the yard. She walked toward him.

"Henry, you gotta forgive me quick. I need you."

He blew a puff of smoke, stubbed out his cigarette, and said, "What's goin' on?"

"May have made an awful mistake with Clara Belle. Ever since she was born, I told her, just be yourself—pay no attention to what people say—stand up for what you know is true—all that shit. And now everybody is talkin' about what a nutcase she is. Jordan's written her off, Dorcas Deputy's saying she's a little heathen and the Virginia Theater's banned her. People've made threatening calls to Mary Faith and Ben Jr., and I didn't even think Harrisonburg had enough Negroes for there to be prejudice. I don't know what to do."

Uncle Henry gathered Aunt Belle in his arms and when he did, she just bawled.

After she calmed down, he asked, "You talked to her lately? Maybe you need to have one of your sessions in the parlor."

"Maybe so."

Clara Belle was grounded for several weeks so the session in the parlor was delayed. When she finally did come up, Aunt Belle was stunned at what she saw. The light that had been in her niece's eyes from day one was gone. In its place was a look of defiance and misery. She wore no bright colored outfit. There was no riddle to start the proceedings, and there would be no Ta-Dah's today.

Clara Belle, without a word, followed Aunt Belle into the parlor. She sat down on the wing chair in the corner.

Aunt Belle started toward the tin box on the desk.

"I d-don't want any more stories," said Clara Belle.

"How about we say the secret words."

She shook her head, and in a voice that sounded like a death knell she said, "You were wrong, Aunt B-Belle, being myself is the worst thing I can be."

Chapter 19

THE TURNING OF THE TABLES

"Now say your five times table," Ben Jr. said.

"But, D-Daddy, fives are too easy. I want to d-do nines."

"That's my girl. Go ahead."

Mary Faith looked from the kitchen to the dining room table where Clara Belle and her dad always did homework together. The two of them had finally found common ground when Clara Belle began to excel in school, especially this year in third grade.

"Nine times zero is zero, nine times one is nine, nine times two is 18, nine times three is 27, nine times four is 36, nine times five is 45, nine times six is 54, nine times seven is 63, nine times eight is 72, nine time nine is 81, nine times ten is 90. Ta—"

"We can do without the Ta-Dah, young lady."

Mary Faith threw down her dishtowel and muttered, "Here we go—"

"How can you do that without stuttering?" he asked.

"I d-don't exactly know. Sometimes it just g-goes away."

"Then try talking slower—and not so loud."

"I'll t-try, Daddy."

"Time to go to school for both you geniuses," said Mary Faith. "Want Daddy to take you down the lane on the way to work, or do you want to walk with Jordan?"

"Ride—Doo-Dah d-doesn't like me anymore."

"Clara Belle, that's not true. He's in seventh grade now and he's—"

"Too d-damn big for his britches."

Clara Belle stomped out of the dining room, down the hall and into her bedroom, slamming the door. Last summer they had added a new master bedroom and bath and gave their room to Clara Belle. Her door had gotten quite a workout.

"Don't you use—"

"Leave her be," said Mary Faith. "She's got enough frustration in her life. Let her get some of it out safely."

They heard something hit the wall.

"*She's* frustrated? What—"

Another thud.

"Isn't it time for your class?"

She knocked on Clara Belle's door.

"Clara Belle, come on—Daddy's leaving."

Clara Belle came out of the room, wearing a glum expression.

As she and her father walked to the car, Mary Faith said, "Miss Heatwole wants to see me right after school. You can play on the playground and then ride home with me."

"Am I in t-trouble again?"

"Get in the car, Clara Belle," said Ben Jr.

She did.

∼

Mary Faith was early. Her days as a schoolteacher had trained her to be one step ahead. Today, she felt a step or two behind sitting there in the school parking lot. She was nervous, as usual. These conferences about Clara Belle always took a lot out of her.

She got out of the car and walked toward the playground. She watched as several boys stood, holding onto the steel rods of the "Wave," while the girls sat around the wooden seat surrounding the pole. The boys swung them high to one side making them scream, and then reversed the motion, bringing the other side down, crashing into the pole in the middle. The girls shrieked as the boys got the Wave going, high tide, low tide, around and around.

She stood there mesmerized until, out of the corner of her eye, she caught sight of Clara Belle coming up the stairs from the lower level. With her was a boy about her age. Mary Faith ducked behind the building and watched.

"Why is your voice so croaky?" taunted the boy. "You sound like a frog—you kiss one?"

Clara Belle sighed, looked around to see if anyone was listening, took a deep breath and began in a weary monotone.

"Almost got it right, turd brain. My cousin and I were catching frogs in my granddaddy's fishpond. I caught one but didn't wash my hands after—went in and had a snack and just like that, my voice changed. Came in handy later when I used my new voice to lure other frogs—kind of like a turkey call."

"That's stupid. I don't believe you," said the boy.

"Who c-cares?" she said and walked away.

Miss Heatwole had been watching, too.

"Time to go in children. The busses are starting to come in. Line up, now, single file."

As Clara Belle walked by Mary Faith, she looked up sadly and shrugged her shoulders.

"D-Don't tell D-Daddy."

~

Mary Faith waited outside Clara Belle's classroom on the second floor until the final bell rang. Five classrooms, third through seventh grade bordered a square landing. The third grade room was at the back-center facing the stairs to the first floor.

Children came bounding out of all five rooms at once, according to which bus they rode—she was almost trampled.

"Come in, Mrs. Miller," said Miss Heatwole. "It's nice to see you. Clara Belle, why don't you go outside and wait with the second bus children. We won't be long."

Mary Faith followed Miss Heatwole into the high-ceilinged room. Rows of pine desks, one immediately behind the other were joined together with black wrought-iron legs. At the front was an oak teacher's desk. To the back were, paned windows reaching almost to the ceiling and giving the whole room a warm, sunny atmosphere. All the rooms on this floor were basically the same. Miss Heatwole's room did have one unique feature—in a corner on the same side as her desk was a multi-colored hooked rug just big enough for a rocking chair and twenty third-grade bodies.

"That's where I tell the Aunt Hepsibah stories," she said, brushing back a stray strand of snow-white hair into the bun at the back of her head.

Mary Faith nodded.

"Please sit down, Mrs. Miller."

She took out a manila folder that seemed too fat for a third grader. She started to open it, then put it down.

"I really don't care much about what that says, you know."

"You don't?"

"She's loud, she fibs, she tells off-color jokes and she curses. All in there, plus what we all know, she's sharp as a tack and funny as a crutch."

Mary Faith had no idea where this was going.

"Nobody ever seems to wonder why she does all those things. Do you, Mrs. Miller?"

"Well, I—"

"I have some ideas—want to hear them?"

"I suppose…sure."

"Any other kid at this school with the wit and brains she has would be sitting pretty. We both know, excuse me for being frank, why she isn't."

Mary Faith's mouth dropped open. No teacher had ever talked to her this way and her first response was to defend Clara Belle as she had always done with everyone. She stopped herself, sensing that something important was about to be said.

"I see I've hit a nerve," said Miss Heatwole, her voice softening and her demeanor changing.

"You have a child who's screaming to fit in some-where—anywhere. She's tried everything she can think of to do that, and she's failing miserably."

"I saw her outside with that boy—"

"She's hurting, Mrs. Miller. On some level you know that already, but I think you've tried so hard to accept her just as she is, that you've done her an injustice."

Mary Faith felt like she'd been hit in the chest with a club. The idea that there was something she hadn't done to help Clara Belle struck such a blow that she couldn't speak.

Miss Heatwole reached over and gently touched her shoulder.

"You've done a wonderful job with Clara Belle. Nobody could have done better. But sometimes it takes a body on the outside to see certain things—somebody who cares almost as much as you do."

Tears stung Mary Faith's eyes.

"I've seen she's been changing," she said. "She's not as happy—there's her cousin Jordan and things at home."

"I don't have to know everything, but you do. Get her to talk to you."

"She's real close to her Aunt Belle," said Mary Faith, "tells her everything."

"See what you can do. Now, there is one thing I can do that might help the stuttering."

"She's been doing that ever since her first word."

"But sometimes—"

"I know; isn't that odd?"

"Maybe we can use it."

Mary Faith didn't understand. She had always tried to ignore the stuttering, not bring any attention to it so Clara Belle wouldn't be self-conscious.

"I don't know," she said. "I don't want to make her feel bad about it, it's just the way she's always been."

"That's what I've been trying to say. There are things we can't change, but we are negligent if we don't change the things we can. I'd be willing to work with her after school a few days a week, if you'd approve. It won't solve everything, but it's a start."

She started to say, "I need to talk with her father" but realized that was ridiculous. Of course he'd think it was a great idea. And for some reason, that bothered her even more.

"Yes, of course, yes," she finally said. "Do we give Clara Belle a choice?"

"No."

~

If it had been anybody but Miss Heatwole, Clara Belle wouldn't have even tried. Aunt Belle had always said to just be herself and part of being herself had always been the way she talked, even if it took awhile sometimes. But her daddy was real excited about this so she learned some tricks Miss Heatwole taught her, and by the end of third grade her stutter was completely gone. She even tried to talk softer, but that was a lost cause. Jordan hadn't even noticed that her stutter was gone—and people thought *she* was retarded.

She and Jordan still walked up the lane but he usually went ahead and she walked with the farm hand's kids. The last Friday before school was out on Monday for the summer, he walked with her.

"I didn't see you much this year," she said in her best new voice.

"Well, you know how it is, my being a seventh grader and all."

"I guess. You should've seen me today. I gave a show you wouldn't believe. I told them about that wooden leg we found up at Aunt Belle's and made up a great story to go along with it about a witchy old lady who—"

"You ever feel bad about all those lies you make up— think about that they know you're lyin'?"

"Who cares—and they're all too dumb to know I'm lying."

What she didn't say was that as soon as her story was over her audience went away and she saw them laughing and looking back at her. She didn't tell Jordan because she was sure he already knew and wasn't doing anything about it. The only time they were ever together anymore was an occasional weekend at Aunt Belle's.

Like he knew what she was thinking, Jordan said, "Guess what Aunt Belle and Uncle Henry got."

"I already know—a television set."

Chapter 20

THE CLOWN APPEARS—DISAPPEARS

When they got to Aunt Belle's, they didn't even ask where Susan and Hank Jr. were. The two of them headed for the living room where Uncle Henry sat in his chair sound asleep, the television still on. All they saw on the screen were lines going in different directions and some letters and numbers—the only thing they heard was an irritating beeping sound.

"Test pattern," Aunt Belle said, starting toward the TV. "Off it goes till something comes on."

"Please leave it on, Aunt Belle, we don't care, we'll watch that. The test pattern is great. Somethin' else'll come on soon," Jordan said.

Hank Jr. came into the room and said, "Come on, you guys, let's go out to the wash house before it gets too dark— nothing to see in here."

Clara Belle and Jordan stared at the screen, waiting. Hank Jr. stomped out of the room.

"Re-Tards."

Finally, the test pattern faded and the announcer gave the call letters of the station. They sat fascinated as they watched the black and white figures move across the eight-inch screen. There was a short weather report and a preview of the night's programs, and by the time the little fizzy guy came on singing the Alka-Seltzer jingle, they were under the spell of that little wooden box.

Suddenly, from somewhere deep inside the box, a man's voice yelled, "Hey, kids, what time is it?" The answer came from a crowd of rowdy kids who screamed at the top of their lungs, "It's Howdy Doody Time!" The clunky-sounding orchestra began to play and was soon joined by the kids singing, "It's Howdy Doody Time, It's Howdy Doody Time..." ending with a cheer, "...so, kids, let's go!"

Clara Belle glanced at Jordan, expecting him to make some pissy comment like "this is so corny," but he didn't take his eyes off the screen.

The announcer said, "And now, boys and girls, here's Buffalo Bob!"

Onto the stage walked a man dressed in a buckskin cowboy outfit with long fringe hanging down the front; the kids went wild, screaming and applauding. Buffalo Bob greeted everyone in what they soon learned was the Peanut Gallery.

He looked out at them and said, "Hello, boys and girls. So glad to see you again."

"He can see us?" asked Clara Belle.

Jordan stared at the TV. He even started answering the questions Buffalo Bob was asking, so Clara Belle decided something magical must be going on.

After visiting with the television audience, Buffalo Bob walked to a ledge.

On the ledge stood a puppet with strings they hadn't even tried to hide—this, they learned, was Howdy Doody. He had a mop of red hair, a freckled wooden face and was dressed in blue jeans and a red and white checked shirt topped off with a neckerchief. Even though she knew he wasn't real, by the time Buffalo Bob talked to him for a few minutes, Howdy Doody was alive.

All at once they heard a toot horn and a clown came on stage. He wore a zebra-striped clown suit with a white ruffled collar around his neck. His face was painted in full clown makeup and fastened around his waist was a box with his name and a toot horn on it. Buffalo Bob greeted him saying, "Hello, Clarabel," and it took Clara Belle less than two seconds to realize that clown's name was the same as hers.

"Did you hear that, Doo-Dah? That c-clown's name is the s-same as m-mine. C-Can you b-beat—"

Jordan was staring at her with a funny look.

She took a deep breath, pretended she was in a show like Miss Heatwole had taught her and said, "*Now* you notice, you shit-brain."

"Language, language," said Uncle Henry, suddenly coming alive.

"I want to hear him talk."

But when Howdy Doody asked him a question, Clarabel only tooted the horn on his box. To answer any and all questions, Clarabel smiled or frowned, or turned his head this way or that, but he did not talk. When someone made him angry, he zapped them with his seltzer bottle and ran off the stage.

When the show was over, Aunt Belle turned the TV off—Clara Belle and Jordan joined Susan and Hank Jr. at the dining room table for the usual supper of Jesse's hot dogs, potato chips and Pepsi.

After the table was cleared, they set up the Monopoly game.

"I'm going to bed," said Clara Belle and left the room with her cousins' mouths hanging wide open.

~

On Monday morning she got up early, ate breakfast in a hurry and went to her room where she stayed until her mother called her. She looked in her mirror at what she had put together. She had dug out the red and yellow clown suit her mother had made for her sixth birthday two years ago. It had been plenty big then and she hadn't grown that much. Around her neck was a long string and at the end was a shoebox with her name printed on the front. She had poofed her frizzy hair out all over her head. She thought about the hat, but the TV clown hadn't had one.

When she came out of the room, her mother's mouth dropped open.

"What in heaven's name are you wearing that for? You can't wear that to school."

"It's costume day," she said and walked quickly out the door. Luckily her father had already gone to work.

She walked right by Jordan's house without stopping. She waited at the end of the lane in the made-over chicken house the farm hands had brought down for bad weather. Jordan didn't see her until the bus pulled out and she walked up beside him to get on.

Before she stepped on the bus, she turned to him and said flatly, "Watch this clown disappear."

By lunchtime everyone was talking about Clara Belle— and Clara Belle the Clown was not talking. Whenever someone asked her a question she'd shake her head and toot the horn she'd taken off her bike. She knew most of the kids had never seen a TV and had no idea who Howdy Doody was—she didn't care.

As Clara Belle had expected, Miss Heatwole went along with her clown act. Not once all day did anyone tease her mute clown about a frog-y-loud voice, thick glasses, strange eyes or her leg brace. No tall tales had to be told to impress, no off-color jokes performed to get a laugh.

Clara Belle stayed mute on the bus all the way home after school.

Jordan got off first and started up the lane without waiting for Clara Belle.

"Jordan?" said Clara Belle.

He started walking faster. She tooted the horn and he turned around.

"I get it now," she said slowly. "I know what I have to do."

BOOK II

THE SEASON OF UNBECOMING

…there are seasons when the tree is dry
and seasons when for the life of us,
the thing looks dead.

Chapter 1

THE DENIAL

This September morning had the feel of that first day of school eight years before, except the feelings were much more complex. Jordan was worried—he was also acutely aware that his concern was not for Clara Belle. His stomach rolled over.

He tooted the horn of his green Ford pickup outside the little house. Aunt Mary Faith had practically gotten down on her knees and begged him to take Clara Belle to school—this, her first day of eighth grade.

In truth, it was a first for all Dayton High students. Until this fall, there had been no eighth grade at all—at the end of seventh grade, you became a freshman in high school and simply moved to the back part of the same building you had been attending for the seven years before.

Clara Belle came down the front steps and walked slowly toward the pickup. The first thing Jordan noticed was how, how…normal she looked. She wore a blue skirt and white blouse with a pink sweater tied by the arms around her shoulders. Her hair had been cut short and her pink/red curls fluffed close to her face. Her horn-rimmed glasses gave her a studious air and her limp was practically unnoticeable. She looked like any other high school girl—though there was the tiny fact that she didn't look much more than ten years old.

All of this Jordan observed with a guilty sense of relief.

"Hey there, Clara Belle," he said as she climbed into the truck. "Ready for eighth grade?"

"Humph," she grunted, slamming the door.

"You guys are the first—"

"Just makes an extra year."

Her voice was still low and coarse, but at least she wasn't yelling at him.

Three years ago, when Jordan had become a freshman in high school, Clara Belle had just finished fourth grade. Then, physically in a completely different part of the building, their contact at school was practically nonexistent. Even at Miller family gatherings he had hung around with Hank Jr. and conveniently avoided her. The changes in Clara Belle today seemed amplified by the distance that had grown between them these past years.

Neither of them said a word the rest of the way to Dayton. When they got to school, Jordan purposely parked in the back parking lot.

"Go ahead in, Clara Belle. I have to stop at the shop building to check on something."

There was an uneasy silence and he could actually see a gray cloud settle on his cousin's face.

"You just don't want to be seen with me, you shit," she said in a tone of voice he'd never heard. "And don't look at me like that. I'll talk anyway I please."

"You always have."

"You know, I actually tried to behave myself for a while after you started ignoring me, but it didn't make any difference. You just went your merry way like you didn't know me—you know how that made me feel?"

"Sorry," he said.

She opened the door and climbed down from the truck. As she slammed the door behind her, she said through the open window, "That's crap. You are not. But you will be."

∼

As Jordan settled into his junior year, he and Clara Belle rarely spoke, even when they saw each other. He was busy with the basketball team and his friends. She was getting involved with some school clubs and was one of the reporters of *The Daytonian,* the school newspaper.

"Have you read this, stud?" said his basketball buddy, Stuart, who held a copy of *The Daytonian* in his hand.

"You made the gossip column, how 'bout that?"

"Give that to me," he said, grabbing the paper out of Stuart's hand.

He looked at the columns titled Local News—School Activities—Editorial—there it was—Dayton Tattletales. He was almost afraid to read.

"That cousin of yours is really full of herself, huh?"

He took a deep breath and read:

"Secret Leaks about Dayton High's Basketball Center. Ask him about playing Joseph in the Garber's Church Christmas pageant."

"Damn her," he said under his breath.

"Well, you gonna leak the secret to your buddy or do I have to go to the source?"

"You wouldn't!"

"No, I wouldn't, but I bet there are plenty of people who will."

Other than the day Clara Belle started school all those years ago, there had never been a longer day. Right before sixth period they passed in the hall and she smiled. Her smile had no twinkle, no fire, no humor.

He quickly walked to his pickup and got in. He didn't want to go home so he drove over to Silver Lake to think.

It wasn't much of a lake actually, more like a large farm pond. But every May when fishing season opened, Silver Lake was the place to be. Cars lined the entire circumference and small boats, filled with men and boys who had been allowed to skip school, floated lazily on the clear silver water. Jordan had been one of those truant boys.

He only wished he could skip school now. He dreaded facing his teammates, the girls who thought he was somebody, his teachers. Would Clara Belle actually tell his secret

or was she bluffing? It really didn't make any difference—
the damage had already been done whether she told or not.
On that first Christmas morning Aunt Belle had asked
him to take care of Clara Belle—she said Clara Belle had
chosen him.

She'd have to choose somebody else.

"I quit!" he said aloud.

~Melinda~

I was in my senior year at Harrisonburg High School,
involved in everything I possibly could be to amass a cred-
ible application for college. My grades were excellent and I
had a good chance of getting into college in North Carolina
after next year. I desperately wanted to go south—there
were some rumblings about a case pending in the Supreme
Court that would finally desegregate schools and I wanted
to be involved in some of the action where I might make
a difference. My parents were only moderately supportive
of my liberal leanings. Aunt Dorcas was predictably horri-
fied, "Melinda, the Bible clearly states that there was nothing at all wrong with slavery and we've certainly given the
Negroes as many opportunities as they can mentally and
socially handle. Leave well enough alone, I say."

"Melinda, see that guy over there? I think you'd like
him. Want me to introduce you?" asked Judy Spruce, a
friend of mine from church who went to Dayton High. This
was the first game of the basketball season and our team
had been beaten by a hair.

"Not in the mood, Jude—when country beats city by
two points in overtime, it is not the time to make new friends
in the enemy camp."

"Oh come on, Mellie, don't be a snob—he's tall, he's
cute, he's a basketball star and he's available."

"OK, I guess—"

I put down my pom-poms on the bleachers and straightened my very sweaty cheerleader uniform.

"I smell like a—"

"He just played a game, what do you think he smells like?"

We walked across the Dayton High gym as the crowd filed out the rear door. As we got nearer the boy Judy had pointed out, I gave him a second look. I'd seen him somewhere but couldn't place him.

"Hey, Jordan, I've got somebody I want you to meet. This is Melinda Dawson, Harrisonburg High's classiest girl."

Jordan—I knew that name.

"Hi," he said, looking down at me, showing no recognition.

"Good game," I said.

"Thanks, you too, I mean—"

"I know what you mean."

"Wanna go to Bar-B-Q Ranch?" asked Judy.

"Sure, I guess. Are you going?" I said, not willing to get stuck by myself with somebody I didn't know.

"Sure—why don't you and Jordan ride with Charlie and me?"

I resisted the temptation to say, "Haven't I seen you someplace?"

As we walked out of the gym, I saw a flash of wild, red hair go by me and out the door—suddenly I remembered.

"That girl over there with the red hair—haven't I seen you with her a couple of times before?" I said.

He glanced over to where I was looking.

"Don't think so," said Jordan. "Must have been somebody else."

Chapter 2

THE HIGH SCHOOL BE-FITTING

Aunt Belle had resigned herself to the "re-do" of her favorite niece as it had gradually developed over the years since Clara Belle had decided to conform. Aunt Belle had understood, she had supported, she had loved, she did not like it one little bit.

The transformation took its toll on her niece, and nobody but Aunt Belle seemed to notice. Their parlor talks had continued, though they weren't much fun for either of them.

"I'm here," the familiar, but subtly altered voice called from the front porch.

"In the parlor," said Aunt Belle.

Clara Belle had called this meeting and had been very mysterious about its purpose.

"Guess what?" Clara Belle said, bounding into the room with a full-mouthed smile.

"Must be good," said Aunt Belle.

"Better than good," she gushed. "Are you ready?"

"Born ready."

"I'm going to be in the band!"

"You're what?…I mean, that's intere…I mean, which—"

"Surprised, huh? Well, Mr. Delbert, the band director, came around to talk to the freshmen and said he needed some volunteers because the band was going to start marching in the Christmas Parade this year—they're gonna get uniforms."

"I'm speechless," said Aunt Belle.

"I'm taking up the piccolo."

"Wouldn't think it'd be a tuba," she said, and was immediately sorry.

"Well, Daddy thought it was a great idea."

"He would..." she said, stopped and tried again. "Clara Belle, I do, too—didn't mean to be flip—just doesn't seem like your kind of thing, that's all."

"Not *your* thing, you mean," said Clara Belle.

"Look, Clara Belle, if this is something you'd enjoy, go at it. You know I just want you to be happy."

"And, I know, 'be myself, be myself'—well, being myself didn't really work that well, now did it?"

"I know how hard—"

"Fitting in isn't half as hard," said Clara Belle, "oughta try it sometime."

Aunt Belle stiffened. She debated whether to go into lecture mode or say something shitty. She took a deep breath and said as cheerily as she could muster, "So what else you up to?"

"Well, I'm in just about everything—I joined any club they let you join as a freshman. Let's see, Future Homemakers of America, the Business Club and, of course, to show my religious side, Tri-Hi-Y. I'm considering trying out for manager of the basketball team for obvious reasons—my chances as a basketball star are nada, but I'd be able to go on all the trips on the bus with the team and I'd get a jacket with a big fat orange and black 'D' and —"

Aunt Belle let her rattle on and on, saying nothing, struggling to not even raise an eyebrow that would suggest she was anything but overjoyed.

"So where exactly do you find a piccolo?" she asked, finally.

"The band has them for rent so I don't have to buy anything if it turns out I can't play. We get fitted for our uniforms on Monday. They're kind of corny looking but a uniform's a uniform—and you know how I always liked dress-ups."

"You wanna borrow some of my earrings?" she said hopefully.

Clara Belle gave her a disgusted look.

"Those days are over, Aunt Belle, it's a no frills world from now on. I'm doing just great being 'Miss Average teenager.' What ain't broke don't need a fixin'. "

Oh, how Aunt Belle wished that were true.

Chapter 3

THE BAND PLAYED ON

Sessions in the parlor had gotten few and far between. Every time Aunt Belle called, Clara Belle had an excuse. She was busy at school and had become involved in more and more but was beginning to complain a little. Maybe that was a good sign. Today she had come up because she had just gotten her driver's license.

"How's 'project fittin'-in' going?"

"Mostly good."

"Enjoyin' band?"

"It's OK. I stuck it out this long because of the new uniforms we got last year," she said to Aunt Belle. "The band is pathetic—can't play, can't march, only people in it are bores. The piccolo was the only instrument Mr. Delbert thought I could play and the sound I get out of it makes me want to scream. Now he's decided that I'm going to represent the band at all-state—shows you how bad the band was if I'm the only choice."

"How 'bout managing the basketball team?"

"Fine, if you like picking up sweaty towels and gathering basketballs after practice. The away games on the bus are fun and I got a big orange and black **D** out of it—looked a little like a chimp in my letter-sweater. Not as cool as I'd hoped."

"Willing to pay the price, are you?"

Clara Belle shrugged.

"Mary Faith says Jordan likes UNC," said Aunt Belle.

"Bully for him."

"Clara Belle, sooner or later you two have to make up. I can't always be your go-between."

"Then don't."

~

"Miss Miller, would you please sight-read this score?"

Mr. Delbert had tried to prepare her but she really was awful at this. Everyone at All-State was required to audition for a position in one of two bands—the Symphony Band or the Concert Band—another name for not-good-enough-for-Symphony Band. She'd already flubbed her major and minor scales.

"May I start again, please?"

She tried again.

"That will be all, Miss Miller, thank you."

The list went up at 11:00 and no surprise, she was in Concert Band, fourth chair piccolo. They practiced all morning and most of the music was still harder than anything the Dayton High Band ever played.

"You having as much trouble as I am with this music?" whispered the girl next to her in fifth chair.

"You too?" she said. "I'm lost."

"Excuse me ladies, is there something you need to say to the group? We're rehearsing here," said the director with a scowl.

"No sir," said the girl, smiling at Clara Belle. When the morning rehearsal was finally over, the girl introduced herself.

"Hi, I'm Ellen Mahoney from right here at Loudan County High—you?"

As quiet as she could make her voice, she said, "Clara Belle Miller—Dayton High."

"Interesting hair—come on into the cafeteria, a bunch of us are eating together."

She followed Ellen into the huge cafeteria—made Dayton High's look like a tearoom.

"Mimi, Susan, this is Clara Belle from...where'd you say?"

"Dayton High—Rockingham County—it's a small school—we have a crummy b… Nice to meet you—you both go to Loudan?"

"No, Nelson County—we're not that good either. We're just here for the boys," Mimi giggled.

"Did you see that cute guy on first trumpet? What a dreamboat—I'd like to toot his horn," laughed Susan.

"What about the guy on snare?" Clara Belle said, hoping he was cute enough to impress the others.

"Oh, yeah, he's cute, too—why don't you 'snare' him for yourself, Clara Belle?"

She smiled, wondering how long it would be until she was found out.

"Hey, Clara Belle, where are you assigned to stay this weekend?"

"A girl called…um … Lettie something, I think. Let me look in my folder… yeah, Lettie Boone, that's it. I met her this morning—she seemed real nice."

Ellen looked at the other girls and rolled her eyes.

"Good grief, you don't want to stay with her," she said. "She's a drip—you see how she dressed? Her family is dirt poor and her house—they live out in the sticks—I don't think they even have an indoor john. Why don't you come to my house? We're all gettin' together for a slumber party."

"But I've already told her I'd meet her after rehearsal. I—"

"Just tell her you knew us from before and didn't know we were gonna be here and you just *have* to stay with us."

This was all new territory—except for the lie, of course.

"OK, I guess I can talk to her after rehearsal."

"We'll meet you under the clock in the hall right after," said Susan. "We'll have a blast."

After rehearsal she met Lettie where they had planned. Clara Belle glanced at her dress—not very becoming, she thought.

"Hi, Clara Belle. Ready to go? My mom's here to pick us up."

"Uh, Lettie. I'm real sorry but…well, you know, I met some girls I knew from before and…well, they invited me to stay with them. Their mother knows my mother and I… I really think it would hurt her feelings if I didn't stay with them. I'm real sorry—maybe next time?"

Lettie's face fell. "Oh," was all she said.

"Well, see you around and thank you for offering to keep me."

Clara Belle turned and walked to the clock where Mimi and Susan were waiting, whispering and giggling. She joined them, quickly blotting from her mind the look on Lettie's face.

After supper in the cafeteria, they went to Ellen's home to change clothes for the evening's activities. Her house was beautiful and sat on a tree-lined city street—obviously, an upper-class neighborhood. Her parents were very welcoming and Clara Belle was pleased at the comfort she felt fitting in with the other girls. She soon forgot that she hadn't planned to stay there from the start or that she hadn't known Ellen and the other girls from before.

They arrived back at the school and went immediately to the gym. For the social that night, the bleachers had been rolled back on both sides of the basketball court to make room for small tables with several chairs around them. On the tables were red and white checked plastic tablecloths—in the center, a small bouquet of plastic flowers. Crepe paper streamers of blue and white were twisted and stretched across the ceiling to hide the large steel rafters and achieve some semblance of atmosphere. The large hanging lights that were necessary to illuminate a basketball game made this difficult. There was no dimming mechanism so certain ones had randomly been turned off to darken the room. What this had created, instead of a cozy, nightclub ambiance, was a patchwork of light and dark that resembled a checkerboard. A disc jockey sat at a table at the far end of the gym, and "Love Me Tender" by Elvis Presley was being played over the large amplifiers.

"We gotta go check our lipstick," said Mimi and left quickly with Susan.

"I'm supposed to meet that guy…oh there he is, see ya," said Ellen and she was also gone, leaving Clara Belle standing in the doorway alone.

She looked around, trying to decide what to do next.

"Clara Belle—that your real name?" said a very tall boy with a dark crew cut.

"Yeah, like the clown and you're…" she looked at his name tag, "Marlin?"

"Like the fish," he laughed.

"Wanna dance?" he asked.

"I never learned. I used to wear…I never learned."

"Come on, I'll teach you."

He was so much taller she felt ridiculous. It was a slow dance.

"Put your left hand on my shoulder here…now I'll put my right arm around your waist, like this…now take my hand up like this. Now, just follow me."

They slowly moved to the middle of the floor. She tried to follow his foot movements but it was hard—his legs were so long.

"Just relax and listen to the music—follow the beat."

She tried, but being stretched out like that was making her limp come back, and she finally said, "Can we just go over and sit down?"

"Sure," he said, "I can talk better than I can dance anyway."

Marlin took Clara Belle's arm and led her to one of the little tables at the edge of the gym. She wondered if she had made a mistake—what in the world would they talk about?

"I saw you when we first got here but didn't see you after auditions," said Marlin.

"You in Symphony?" she asked.

"Uh-huh—"

"That's why—I'm in Concert—messed up my scales big-time."

"They're tricky, for sure—maybe next year."

She was surprised when the conversation settled into a familiar, easy flow of chitchat. They talked about their families, their schools and their interests.

"I play baseball on my high school team," he said.

"Really, what position?"

"Short stop."

"Little tall, aren't you?"

He laughed and it felt good to have that old familiar kind of response for a change.

Her mind began to wander when Marlin started going into detail about the game of baseball. She was very pleased with herself—she hadn't been this comfortable talking with a boy since—

She looked at her watch.

"Look at the time—I think I'd better catch up with the girls I'm staying with tonight," she said.

"May I have your address? We could write."

"Sure, I'll give it to you tomorrow."

She went looking for Ellen and found her snuggled up in a corner with trumpet boy.

"I'll meet you in the hall—my dad'll be here in five minutes," Ellen said, dismissing her.

When they got in the car, Mimi said, "Who was that weird looking guy you were talking to all night?"

"Just a guy I met."

"Looked like an ape. Sorry you got stuck—that happens sometimes."

The next day after the concert Clara Belle saw Lettie standing alone in the hallway. She was almost in front of her, ready to tell her she was sorry, when Ellen intercepted her.

"You don't really want to do that," she hissed through a nasty grin and guided Clara Belle out the door.

What was it that Aunt Belle had said about paying the price?

Chapter 4

THE GOLDEN GOOSE

The faculty of Dayton High School didn't quite know what to make of Preston Charles "Mack" McDonald III— he discovered that immediately. After all, he was from "out west somewhere" and as Miss Wilson, the typing teacher, had said, "You look way too young to be a teacher." Of course, the average age of the teachers at Dayton was fifty and most of them had been there for twenty years. Mack had graduated from the University of Colorado at twenty and earned his Master's degree in English before his twenty-third birthday. That was another thing that made him suspect—teachers at Dayton had bachelor's degrees.

The students were another story. They had taken to him right away, happy to have an adult at school who knew who Elvis Presley and Buddy Holly were—he much preferred Bach and Hayden but kept that under his hat.

His first exposure to Clara Belle Miller was an editorial she had written in *The Daytonian*, the school newspaper, of which she was editor. The article was about the plight of the American Indian, an issue in which he had been interested but couldn't imagine a high school student caring a whit about—they all still thought General Custer was a hero.

"It's very nice to meet you, Clara Belle. I've been impressed with your writing in *The Daytonian*. I don't believe I've had you in any of my classes."

She was much smaller than he expected—her writing seemed so...well...big—she couldn't have been more than five feet.

"No, sir, but I'm signed up for your creative writing class this semester."

"That's good. You have some insightful ideas and a unique style. I'll look forward to working with you. I especially liked the piece on the American Indian."

"You're from out west, aren't you? What are you doing here in this hick town?"

Her slanted blue eyes were as piercing as her voice and the direct question she posed.

"Long story."

"Well, I sure can understand your wanting to get away from home. I'm planning to get the hel... heck out of here as soon as I graduate."

"Anyone ever told you that you have a stage voice, a voice for drama?"

"I've been called a drama queen before, but no, most people used to tell me my voice drives them crazy."

"Maybe they just can't see potential."

Her slanted eyes viewed him suspiciously.

"Tell me about your interest in Native Americans. Where did you get your information on General Custer?"

Her face brightened.

"I have an aunt who knows a lot about Indians. She'd always wondered about the tales of how great the General was so I wrote a paper for history class. Found out he was a solid-gold jerk—a real wacko—killed, what'd you call them?"

"Native Americans. In Colorado some of them are using that term now."

"I like it...anyway, Custer was the 'show no mercy-take no prisoners' poster child. The In...Native Americans didn't stand a chance. I used to go to cowboy movies with my...I went to cowboy movies and while everybody else was cheering for the cowboys, I was feeling sorry for the Indians."

"Unusual response for a kid."

"I used to be weird," she said.

The bell rang.

"I have to go."

"Very nice talking with you, Clara Belle. See you in class."

"Sixth period, right?"

"Right," he said.

~

"I'm staying after today—Mr. McDonald has a proposition for me."

"You're spending an awful lot of time with him—are you sure his intentions are honorable?" said Mary Faith, smiling.

"Just interested in my mind, Mom—my incredible mind. He thinks I have insightful ideas and a unique style."

"Well, isn't that nice."

Clara Belle rolled her eyes, "Good grief, Mom, you're beginning to sound like Daddy."

This had been going on all of Clara Belle's junior and senior years. Clara Belle would write an article for the school paper or for class and she and Mr. McDonald would get together after school and hash it out. Most of the time they were on the same side of an issue, but not always—sometimes she'd come home furious that he couldn't see things her way.

Mary Faith had met him. He wasn't actually handsome but there was something about him. He was short with a slight build, but solid looking. His brown hair was curly, almost kinky and his clothes looked like he'd slept in them. His eyes had the same steely blue and intensity as Clara Belle's and he wore glasses. He talked both with his hands and his whole body—at first she thought he was nervous around her but decided it was just that he was animated and excited about his subject. Passionate was not a word she wanted to use to describe someone who was with her daughter so much, but that's the only one that fit. After she talked with him, she felt comfortable that he had Clara

Belle's best interest in mind. Mary Faith was grateful—Clara Belle seemed unusually happy.

~

"I think you ought to use that paper you wrote for class on the Civil Rights Movement in *The Daytonian*—rewrite it as an editorial," said Mack.

"You sure? I told you about the last time I stated my views on that issue. My Aunt Belle turned me into a bleeding liberal at the age of five. She was a fountain of radical information on every social issue."

Clara Belle's face clouded over.

"I can't believe you even thought about things like that at such a young age—they really ban you from the Virginia Theater?" he said cautiously.

"Not a great time in my life."

He waited for her to say something else—she was finished.

"That was then—the movement is further along now. A little consciousness raising wouldn't hurt."

"Kids around here have no consciousness to raise. We don't have a single black person at Dayton High—not because they aren't allowed, but because we don't have any around here."

"Work something up—talk to your Aunt Belle—I'll censor it so they won't ban you from school."

She laughed weakly. There were moments when he saw humor lurking behind those eyes but she always kept it in check.

"You said you had a proposition," she said.

"I do. Remember when I first met you I said you had a voice for the theater?"

"I thought you were just shi… trying to—"

He noticed she often had difficulty expressing herself without resorting to cursing, an old habit she was obviously

140

trying to subdue. As a high school teacher, he was familiar with the dilemma.

"I say what I mean. I've been asked to direct the senior play and I wondered if you might want to try out. It's a comedy called "Brother Goose" and there's a part in it that I think would be perfect for you."

"I don't do comedy."

"That's not what I heard—I've been talking to Miss Heatwole."

"Uh-oh."

"Clara Belle the Clown. Has a nice ring to it, don't you think?"

"That was a long time ago, before… before—"

"Before you decided to conform? Clara Belle, from what I hear, you have a gift you've been hiding under a bushel for some years."

"A lot safer under there."

"But not nearly as much fun. Here," he said, handing her a script, "read this over—look at the part of Hyacinth, see—"

"Hyacinth, did you say Hyacinth?"

"Hy, they call her. She's the kid sister who runs around in a football helmet all the time. I think you'll like her."

"Football helmet, huh? Does sound intriguing—think it'd fit over my hair?"

∼

"What's this?" said Mary Faith as she picked up the small, blue, paperback book.

"Script," said Clara Belle.

"To what?"

"The senior play—Mr. McDonald wants me to try out."

"Are you?"

"Probably not."

"Because?"

Clara Belle walked over to the window and looked out.

"It's a dumb part—some tomboy girl who wants to play football and runs around the whole play with a helmet on. Daddy would be mortified."

"Sounds cute to me."

"Cute's a four-letter word, Mom."

Clara Belle had read the play. She had recited the lines alone in her room and had laughed out loud. It really was funny—she could almost see herself on the stage being Hy, having the audience laugh and applaud the way they had when she was Clara Belle the Clown a lifetime ago. There was another part of her that remembered a different kind of laughing—she couldn't be positive which this kind might turn out to be. And, she had to consider her father—he would think being in a play was frivolous and stupid—a waste of good studying time.

Tryouts were the next day after school. She'd decide later.

She couldn't sleep and the next morning she had diarrhea. By sixth period she still hadn't decided and the little blue book kept staring at her all during creative writing class.

"See you at tryouts," said Mr. McDonald as the final bell rang.

"I don't—"

"Be there!"

She walked from the classroom against the tide of students heading down the hall toward the buses. She came to the big double doors leading to the gymnasium. She took a deep breath and went in. At the end of the gym was a small stage—the heavy velvet curtain was open and on the stage was a circle of chairs. Several students were already there talking to Mr. McDonald. She started up the set of stairs to the right of the stage. Mr. McDonald saw her.

"Come on up," he said.

"I'll be right back," she said, running to the girls' locker room. She sat in the stall, her stomach churning.

"Crap," she said under her breath and suddenly laughed. "Ain't that the truth."

She felt a little better and headed back to the stage, where almost all the chairs were now filled with her classmates. She had known nearly all of these kids since first grade. There were the ones who had ignored her, teased her and/or laughed at her. A few of them from band and *The Daytonian* staff had become friends of sorts but, all in all, as she walked to her chair, she felt like an outsider—an intruder.

"Clara Belle, have a seat and turn to page 47 in the script. You read Hy's part, Johnny you read Jeff, and Bobby you read the truck driver."

As they began reading the lines, Clara Belle was suddenly calm—little by little something else started to happen—she felt herself melt away and she *became* Hyacinth. She was no longer reading the lines but had the sense that she was making them up as she went along. For quite some time she didn't even notice the laughter coming from the rest of the students sitting around the circle. It was finally a great guffaw from Mr. McDonald that brought her back to the moment and the rest of the students spontaneously applauded as she put down the script that she hadn't used for five pages.

Chapter 5

THE COMMAND PERFORMANCE

"Dear Jordan," the note said, "Clara Belle is in her senior play at Dayton on Friday afternoon. Your mom says you'll be home for fall break. Be there!! Aunt Belle."

"Melinda, you've just got to go with me," Jordan pleaded over the phone. "Aunt Belle says I have to go and I need someone to run interference—you could finally meet her face to face."

"Jordan, you ought to do this yourself," Melinda said. "It's about time you made up with that cousin of yours—I'll meet her later."

Through their off and on relationship over the past four years Jordan had gradually filled Melinda in on his whole history with Clara Belle—she had told him hers. Now they were engaged to be married the summer after they graduated—Melinda from NC State, he from UNC. They were home on fall break.

"Melinda, please," he said.

"I'll make a deal with you," Melinda said. "I'll meet you there, but not till after the play's over and you've had a chance to see her by yourself first. She know you're coming?"

"Aunt Belle may have told her—I don't know what to expect—we've been on the outs for so long."

"Then it's time," Melinda said. "It's time."

~

As he walked into the Dayton High School gymnasium, he felt as though he had never left—nothing had changed. Even the smell was the same—they'd just put a new coat of wax on the floor. Covering the painted lines on the freshly buffed basketball court were several hundred folding chairs, now filling with parents, teachers and older students. Little folks from the elementary grades filed in, carrying wooden chairs from their classrooms, and took their places nearest the stage.

For twelve years this space had been the center of his life outside the Miller family. On his little wooden chair he had watched as they were entertained by children's plays and bored by motivational speakers during assemblies. From the wooden bleachers, season after season, he had watched as the older boys practiced basketball, waiting for the day when he would be old enough to try out for the team. In the classrooms bordering the gym, Jordan had painfully learned to type ten words a minute, struggled with second year Spanish and checked out books for term papers from the inadequate little library. He had tried, with little success, to master the elements chart which hung high on the wall of chemistry lab—he was successful learning the secrets of the Haunted House in that same room the Halloween of his junior year.

As the teachers filed in behind their classes, nearly all were familiar faces. Miss Effie managed a quick wave in the middle of her effort to keep the unruly second graders in line. Mr. Mills, wearing the same gray suit and red bowtie he'd worn for his twenty-five years as principal, approached him with a big smile and an outstretched hand.

"How are things going in Tar Heel country?" he said.

"Just fine, Mr. Mills, but I miss playing basketball," Jordan answered. "I thought I was pretty good here, but when I tried out down there, I didn't stand a chance."

"Well, hello there, Jordan…Jordan Glick, isn't it?" said a voice behind him. He turned around.

"Miss Heatwole, my goodness are you sti…uh …really good to see you. I've never forgotten my times tables or Aunt Hepsibah stories. Third grade was my favorite year in elementary school."

"Why thank you—that's mighty nice."

She paused.

"Jordan, you must be here to see Clara Belle perform. She's come a long way since her Clara Belle the Clown routine."

Why did he feel like she was scolding him?

He searched for a seat, then saw Aunt Mary Faith and Uncle Ben Jr. sitting way in the back. He took the seat next to them.

"Well, Jordan, here we go again," whispered Uncle Ben Jr. Aunt Mary Faith glared at him.

Just then the house lights began to dim and the stage lights were turned up. The curtain opened—there were several students on the stage but no Clara Belle. The play began; Jordan squinted to see the program. There it was— Hyacinth—Clara Belle Miller. Suddenly he heard her voice. Out from the wings came a little kid dressed in an oversized football jersey and wearing a football helmet. From the moment she hit the stage, she was the center of attention. Each time she exited, the energy on stage diminished, the pace slowed—the minute she made another entrance, everything geared up a notch or two. Her effect on the other students in the play was electric and they became more animated and involved when she was interacting with them. She fired each line with perfect timing and the audience was howling at her antics.

At the curtain call each actor took his or her bow. When it was her turn, Clara Belle came to center stage and bowed very professionally. The crowd began cheering and chanted, "Clara Belle, Clara Belle." Clara Belle took off her football helmet, raised her hands in the air and shouted, "TA-DAH." The audience erupted with a sound that rivaled a final basket at a DHS game. Aunt Mary Faith and Jordan were standing, applauding with the rest of the audience—Uncle Ben Jr. sat stone-faced.

As the students went back to their classrooms and the parents and guests filed out, Clara Belle came running up to Jordan with a young man in tow. She was flushed and excited.

"Doo-Dah, this is Mr. McDonald, my English teacher. He's the one who directed the play. Mr. McDonald, this is the cousin I told you about. This is Doo-Dah."

"Clara Belle, you were amazing. Nice to meet you, Mr. McDonald."

Jordan shook his hand.

"Thanks, Doo-Dah, I…wait, there's Dad…never mind," she sighed. "He's leaving."

"Ahem, Jordan," Melinda said from behind him.

"Oh, Melinda, you're here—Melinda, this is my cousin Clara Belle Miller, Clara Belle, this is my fiancée."

"So-o-o… you liked my performance did you, *Jordan?*" Clara Belle said, narrowing her eyes at Melinda.

Jordan shrugged his shoulders and gave Melinda a weak smile.

"I have to get back to my classroom, Clara Belle," said Mr. McDonald. "Great job—see you tonight."

"Jordan, I really ought to get back home," Melinda said. "Mom and I haven't visited much. I'll take the car and you can call me when you two have caught up."

Jordan gave her a desperate look.

"Melinda, can't you do that later?" asked Jordan. "I've hardly seen you since we've been home and we have to go back—"

"Have a good chat—really good to finally meet you, Clara Belle."

"Jordan told you tales about me, huh?" she said sharply.

"No… I mean…well, yes but…I uh…let's just say… we'll talk sometime. See you later, Jordan."

Chapter 6

THE SAME OLE SAME OLE

"Why don't we go up to the barn—neutral territory?" Jordan said. He wasn't looking forward to this—and he was back to being a little mad at Clara Belle. Why did she act that way with Melinda?

"Let's walk," Clara Belle said.

They walked in silence up the lane toward Granddaddy Miller's—past the limestone wall surrounding the small Mennonite graveyard where they'd read the names and dates on the faded tombstones—past the sales' barn where they'd acted out movies they saw at Saturday matinees. On the top of the hill they stopped and looked out over the farm that stretched in all directions.

Massanutten Peak looked so blue today jutting up in the distance.

"Not a bad view for free, huh," she said.

"I'd forgotten," he said.

They continued on down the other side of the hill as the old house came into view.

"Want to stop and say hi to Granddaddy?" he said, hoping to delay this as long as possible. "He's sort of lonesome since Grandmother Miller died."

"She's probably still there haunting the place, wielding her broom stick."

They knocked on the door, but no one answered.

"Probably napping," said Jordan.

They walked up to the barn.

"I miss Moses—always sounded like he was yelling 'Help! Help!' " Clara Belle said.

"Died too, huh?" Jordan said.

She nodded.

Jordan slid open the large, wooden door and the light poured in. As they entered, they both looked up at the hay-loft—neither of them spoke.

"That OK?" she finally said.

"Sure."

They climbed up the ladder. The fat hemp rope still hung from the rafter at the top. Clara Belle grabbed it and handed it toward him.

"I pass—was always scared to death of that thing," he said.

"You never told me that."

"Didn't tell you everything."

"Good fake," she said, releasing the rope.

They each selected a bale and sat down, waiting for the other to start.

He picked a straw from the bale and put it in his mouth.

"You really were good today, Clara Belle," said Jordan. "Where was Aunt Belle?"

"Thanks—we've got another performance tonight—I told her to wait till I got one under my belt."

"She'll love it."

"I guess."

Silence.

"I...," they both said at the same time.

"You go ahead," Jordan said.

She took a deep breath.

"I am sorry, the *Daytonian* thing—it was a shitty thing to do but—"

"I'm sorry, too, ... I sorta deserv—"

"True...well, a little...but...I never told, you know."

"Figured you didn't. It was your fault, you know, that I peed down my Joseph robe—that damn long speech...and I just got so tired of...well, you know. "

"Just say it, Doo-Dah. I was a pain in the butt."

149

"Well, yes...not always...I did my share of being a...I still wonder sometimes why you kept on trying to stay close."

"That's easy—I had no choice after Aunt Belle told me that you chose me," said Clara Belle.

"What do you mean, 'I chose *you*?' " asked Jordan.

"She never told you? One day in the parlor, real early on, she said that we were going to be special cousins to each other, that there were things I could teach you and things you could teach me. She said I was lucky that you *'chose'* me."

"I'll be damned," said Jordan. "She told me exactly the same thing about you choosing me. Sly old fox—hooked us from the beginning."

They both relaxed a little. Clara Belle smiled.

"Really nailed you on the snipe hunt."

"I *did* deserve that one."

Silence.

"Remember the wood—"

"The wooden leg," he laughed, "boy, did we ever make a big deal about that. Never did figure out who it belonged to, did we? Where'd we finally put it?"

"Don't remember."

Silence again.

"So you're gettin' married?"

"Uh-huh, Melinda's a great girl—oughta get to know her."

"Cheerleader-type—never figured you'd end up with a fluff-head."

"What's wrong with you anyway, Clara Belle? You were pissy to her at the play."

"Was not—"

"Were too—"

"Now, that sounds real grown up, you...you...fart-head-stick-in-the-mud," said Clara Belle.

"Some things just never change—are we finished here?"

"Completely!"

Chapter 7

THE MILLER BREAKFAST— REVISITED

~Melinda~

Before Jordan and I went back to school, the Millers planned a gathering to celebrate our engagement. Naturally, it was held in Granddaddy Miller's house on the farm and the aunts had decided to recreate the Christmas breakfast, which hadn't been held since Grandmother Miller died.

We got into the 1950 VW van I talked Jordan into buying just before we graduated. It met his need for a vehicle, the price was right, and it satisfied my latent beatnik streak. On the way there, Jordan finally told me about his conversation with Clara Belle in the barn after the play.

"Jordan, I can't believe it. You two were supposed to make up."

"We did—for about five minutes," Jordan replied.

I waited for him to say something more——he was finished.

"She actually called me a fluff-head?"

He shrugged, "What can I say?"

"I'm asking her to be in the wedding, Jordan—period," I said. "With your history, I can't believe you wouldn't want to."

"And with the way she's acted the few times we've been together, I can't believe you do," Jordan fired back.

"Let's just say that I understand what's going on and I know we can work this out between the two of us. And don't forget *our* history, Clara Belle and me—she was my inspiration—we go way back—she just doesn't know it yet."

~

No matter what changes there had been through the years, breakfast at Granddaddy Miller's always smelled exactly the same to Jordan.

As he walked in the front door with Melinda at his side he was bombarded by the aromas: bacon and sausage frying in the iron skillets, buttered toast with burnt crumbs on cookie sheets in the oven alongside the ever popular "scalped" oysters.

"Boy, does this smell good," said Melinda, reading his mind.

"I'll take your coat in the bedroom," he said. He walked into Granddaddy Miller's bedroom where the coats were piled high. There was no white wicker basket, but the memory of it was still vivid.

He put the coats on the bed and rejoined Melinda in the front hall. They walked into the living room where Granddaddy Miller sat in his wing chair in front of the fireplace—Grandmother Miller's chair was empty. There was no little cedar tree in the corner and no presents spilling out into room. They walked over to Granddaddy Miller.

"Well, Chordan, is it? Yah, Chordan, who is this young lady you bring here, yet?"

"Granddaddy Miller, this is my fiancée, Melinda. We're going to be married in June when we graduate from school."

"From high school, much too young to get hitched."

"Granddaddy, we're both graduating from college this year," said Jordan, smiling at Melinda.

"Hmm, this makes a body feel old and befuddled. Melinda, is it?"

"Yes, sir," said Melinda.

"This a good boy, this Chordan."

"Yes, sir, he is. Very nice to meet you. I—"

"I'm too young for you to be gettin' married," greeted Uncle Henry as he pounded Jordan on the back. He glanced at Melinda, "Must be the little filly—sassy, Jordan, very sassy."

"Uncle Henry, this is Melinda, Melinda, Uncle Henry—where's Aunt—"

"Hey shite-poke, how's tricks?" Aunt Belle, this year a brunette, made her entrance with her laundry basket—there were no gifts wrapped in comics, only the food she was bringing for the breakfast. She gave him a perfunctory hug, grunted at Melinda and went straight to the kitchen.

"Are Susan and Hank…?" he started, but Uncle Henry was already gone to find his smoking buddies out back.

As more and more Millers arrived and were introduced to Melinda, he began looking around for Clara Belle. He knew Melinda was plotting to get them together without a fight and she also was determined to ask her to be in the wedding. He knew she was right and deep down he wanted to be on good terms with his cousin again. Time to grow up, as Melinda put it.

Aunt Mary Faith and Uncle Ben Jr. came through the door and Jordan looked for Clara Belle. She wasn't with them so he went out back with the smoking uncles and his now smoking cousins, Hank Jr. and Susan. Melinda followed Aunt Mary Faith into the kitchen.

"Melinda, welcome to trial-by-family," said Mary Faith. "We all had to pass Christmas breakfast at Granddaddy Miller's before we could join the clan," she said. "I'm really pleased for you and Jordan."

"Thanks, Mary Faith, …uh …where's Clara Belle?"

"She may or may not come—you know how she is—or maybe you don't?"

"I've heard a few—"

"Ta-Dah," came the pronouncement from the front hall.

"Well," said Mary Faith, shaking her head, "there you go."

"Come on, Melinda," said Jordan, "let's eat—and we don't even have to sit at the children's table."

"Can't believe all this food," I said, watching as the aunts brought in platters of eggs, bacon, sausage, toast, hot curried fruit and scalloped oysters. Jordan took a large portion of the oysters.

"Thought you hated those slimy things," said Aunt Belle.

"I finally learned to like them. They have this course at UNC called 'appreciating mollusks.' "

"For a fart-head-stick-in-the mud, that was excellent humor," said Clara Belle, who had just come into the dining room.

I saw Jordan stiffen.

Clara Belle waited a beat, gave him that grin, and then she winked.

Jordan shook his head, smiled a weak grin and said quietly, "Ta-Dah."

After breakfast Jordan went off with his cousins again and as the aunts began to clear the table, I saw Clara Belle standing alone.

"Clara Belle, is there a quiet place where we can talk?" I asked.

"I guess so...sure, let's go to one of the upstairs bedrooms."

They walked up the back staircase from the dining room. There was a landing at the top and a door opening to a bedroom.

"This was Aunt Belle's room," Clara Belle said. "Her stepmother, the Grandmother Miller I knew, used to stand on the landing waiting for her with the frying pan because Aunt Belle never would clean up her room."

Clara Belle opened the door, "As a Miller, you have to put up with the family stories—it's required."

We went into the room—Clara Belle sat down on the antique, knotty-pine bed. I went to the chair in the corner.

"Jordan says you were great in the play."

"Most everybody seemed to think so."

"Clara Belle, I have an important question to ask you, but first I need to… for a long time I've…I—"

"You want my permission to marry Doo-Dah, right?"

At first I thought she was serious and then she did what I had just seen her do with Jordan—what she had done that night at the Christmas pageant—her grin started as a twinkle in her eye, moved down to her mouth and then she winked.

"You did that the first time I ever saw you—you winked at your Aunt Belle at Garber's Church."

"You were there?" she said as her blue eyes widened.

"And other places, too. I've been a fan of yours since I was ten years old."

BOOK III

THE SEASON OF BECOMING

"Everything has a deep dream of itself
and its fulfillment."

Chapter 1

THE KLEINE CLOWN—REVISITED

Clara Belle looked in the mirror.

"Perfect," she said aloud.

She had dragged out the clown suit her mother had made for her sixth birthday party. The red and yellow outfit was a little faded and a little small, but the effect was still there. She had let her hair grow out to a length that she could pick with a comb to a clown-wig frizz. She had painted her face with clown makeup she had bought at Glen's Fairprice. Her own outrageous grin was exaggerated with red and white with a black outline. A teardrop in black fell from one of her eyes in stark contrast to the smile on her lips—a stroke of artistic genius and deep metaphorical significance.

"I'll show those prissy, boring, all-girl-school bitches!" she said to her reflection.

She left her dorm room and walked the back way to morning convocation. She was to lead the morning prayer. She went in the back door and waited for everyone to get in. The faculty and seniors had already processed in their pompous academic finery to the hymn, "God of Our Fathers."

"Our Invocation will be given by freshman, Clara Belle Miller."

Clara Belle walked to the podium—there were gasps from those on stage and expressions of disbelief from those in the pews.

"Let's all bow our heads," she said in her most Clara Belle voice.

"God and I have this little joke. I say, 'What's invisible and smells like carrots,' and God says, 'I know that one—Bunny Farts!' "

"Ta-Dah!" she ended and raised both her arms with a defiant grin.

There was not a sound from anyone in the audience. The Dean of the College came to the podium and said, "Miss Miller, pack your bags and leave this campus."

The entire student body and faculty turned its back and walked out of the chapel, leaving her there alone on the podium in her clown outfit.

Clara Belle's heart was pounding and she was sweating profusely as she opened her eyes and looked around. The upstairs bedroom at Aunt Belle's was still pitch black—she looked at the clock—three a.m.

"Shit," she said.

~

When the night finally ended, she went down to the kitchen where Aunt Belle was already putting out the donuts and hot chocolate.

"Mornin', Sunshine, how's…Good Lord, you look like you've been run over by a Mack truck."

"Something like that—had a rough night," said Clara Belle.

"Wanna talk about it?"

"Yes and no."

"When you decide which, let me know—eat."

"Not hungry."

"What's your point?"

Clara Belle picked up a donut, then put it down.

"Isn't there an old wive's tale that says if you tell your dreams before breakfast, they'll come true?"

"Is it one you want to?"

"Don't think so—but I'll wait anyhow."

She drank her hot chocolate and ate a donut.

"Before I tell you the dream, I need to tell you about my conversation with Jordan's Melinda at Granddaddy's when they were getting engaged."

"I'm listenin'."

"Well, I was pretty pissy to her right after the senior play and Jordan and I tried to make up but that didn't go real well because he was pissed at me."

"Sounds familiar."

"But she just blew it off like she didn't care what I'd said and wanted to talk with me."

"Asked you to be in the wedding, right?"

"Yes, but that was after."

Aunt Belle waited as Clara Belle fiddled with her cup.

"Aunt Belle," she finally began, "Melinda said she'd been watching me do my thing for a long time."

"What thing is that?"

"You know... Uh... the thing I did before I... stopped."

"Oh, *THAT* thing."

"She was there when I did the Christmas pageant, she was at the Virginia Theater, and she was at Bible school when her Aunt Dorcas dubbed me a little heathen. She even knew how Jordan had given up on me and understood how that made me feel."

"So—?"

"Well, she... she...liked it—she said she, to use her words, 'admired my spunk.' "

"And how did that make you feel?"

"Jeez, Aunt Belle, you sound like a friggin' shrink!"

"Sorry...so what are you sayin'?"

"I got to thinking about the fitting-in thing and wondering how I could maybe be both...you know...do what you always wanted me to do and still not drive everyone crazy. Like when I go to Southampton Monday and am with all those proper southern belles."

"And—?"

"I decided I didn't know how, but maybe I could try."

"Sounds like a plan," said Aunt Belle with a big smile.

"That's where my dream last night comes in...I don't think I...I just can't...I got this full academic scholarship that Daddy set up and he's so pleas....I just can't, that's all."

"So if you've already decided, why are you tellin' me?"

"Because...Oh, never mind."

"I have only one thing to say about the issue...may I?"

"You will anyway."

"Remember me asking you a long time ago when you were starting school whether you remember the first words we said together?"

"My first word was 'Doo-Dah.' "

"Before that...with me...here in the parlor."

Clara Belle looked out the window avoiding Aunt Belle's steady gaze.

"I remember when I stopped saying it—I remember why."

"The words were from a Psalm—switched it around a little it was...'thank-you G—' "

Clara Belle got up from her chair and started upstairs to get her things.

"My dream tells me otherwise—I choose to consider it a warning and say 'thank you, God' for that."

"What about Melinda—what about spunk?" yelled Aunt Belle after her.

"Spunk'll just have to wait."

Chapter 2

THE FITTING IN—ACT II

The last thing her father had said when he let her off at the dorm and unloaded her stuff was, "I know you'll make us all proud." And she had every intention of doing just that.

She had found it easy to forget her conversation with Melinda—she found it easy to forget Aunt Belle's secret words. Forgetting her last conversation with Mr. McDonald was a little more difficult. After her valedictory address he had come over to the little house for the after-graduation party. He stayed until most everybody else had left and they went out to the front porch.

"This is where I first gave the name, Doo-Dah, to Jordan," she said absently.

Talking to him out of school seemed awkward and she didn't know quite how to be.

"Good speech," he said.

"All BS and you know it—a complete sell-out."

"Ah, yes, but very well delivered."

"True."

"So, you're going to the sunny south to school—an all-girls' school, no less."

"I guess Daddy thought I might pick up a little southern grace and manners there."

"I looked it up. Southampton has a good academic program and you'll be right in the middle of the civil rights activism. You ought to do well there—get involved. Have any idea what you want to study—what you want to do?"

"Survive," she said.

"Clara Belle Miller, from the little I've learned about you from this last year, you better damn well do more than that. You can't bury that spirit of yours forever."

Those kinds of statements reminded her of Aunt Belle so she lumped them in that category and filed them away with the rest.

~

Clara Belle toed the line, which really turned out to be fairly easy. The rules at Southampton were so archaic and strict that if you went by the little white handbook they gave out the first of the year, you fit in. There was a dress code—no Bermuda shorts or jeans outside on campus, only in the dorms—for classes, skirts and blouses or dresses—for teas and other college functions, hats and white gloves. There was no dating for freshmen, except on date nights, Friday and Saturday, and then only a double date with an upperclassman. There was to be no talking with a male after 6:30 p.m.—not that there were many males to talk to except the upperclassmen's dates. If you went off campus, you needed a really good reason and were required to sign in and sign out on a card at a designated area. Curfews were strict and being late or any other infraction of the rules subjected you to a visit to residence counsel, a mini-court where fellow students sat in black robes over their pajamas and decided whether you had a good excuse or would be disciplined accordingly. Quiet hour began at 8:00 PM and ended at breakfast the next morning. There was little wiggle room and that, for Clara Belle, worked extremely well.

Her roommate, Sandra Gilman, was a tall girl from New York State who had gone to a prep school. Her experience there had taught her the invaluable skills of smoking and playing bridge. Oddly enough, there were no rules in the little white book about smoking so, in the Tower Room, late into the night, girls sat in their pajamas and filled the room with smoke, bridge and girl talk. Clara Belle soon joined them in bridge playing and smoking—she faked the girl talk. There was some sense of satisfaction that her father would not have approved of the Tower Room.

In academics, Clara Belle was, as always, an excellent student. She made dean's list grades the first grading period and was elected Class of '62 secretary. She avoided thorny discussions about social issues and religion and kept a low enough profile that she wasn't tempted to do anything weird. When she was asked to give the invocation at chapel, she graciously declined.

Chapter 3

THE SEASON FOR RATTING

CRAVOTTA! That's what everyone called her—just, CRAVOTTA! Perhaps it was because her name, Amanda Louise, just didn't begin to fit. More likely the reason was that CRAVOTTA!, pronounced with capital letters and an exclamation point at the end, summed up her larger-than-life personality. She was almost as short as Clara Belle and her dark, black hair framed her face like a football helmet. Her dark eyes were oddly shaped and big as marbles—they appeared to be in a constant state of amazement. Her mouth, which seemed to have far too many teeth, was large for her small face—when she smiled there was a sense that she knew something no one else knew—and she wasn't telling.

The first time Clara Belle encountered Cravotta in action was during "Rat Week" at Southampton, a benign and mostly fun experience of hazing by the sophomores. The intensity of the present year's hazing depended on how the former freshmen's ratting had gone. If the upper classman had a positive experience the year before, the ratting was good-natured and only mildly humiliating. After all, Southampton had the reputation of being a well-respected, southern comfort, lady-like college. However, if a student felt that she had been treated unfairly and the memory was still lurking, there could be hell to pay for the rising freshmen.

Besides wearing the traditional freshmen "beanies" with the class colors, there were songs, poems and other material that a Rat was required to memorize for regurgitation at the whim of any given sophomore at any given moment of day or dead of night. The purpose of much of the memorization was to drill rules and traditions of the school into freshmen brains for future use.

Clara Belle found the whole exercise confusing from her personal perspective. On one hand, she knew that the humiliation was staged and not meant to actually bring anyone down. On the other hand, her own early experiences had made her sensitive to mockery of any kind.

"Rat Miller, recite the proclamation pledge and sing the '61 song," yelled one of the sophomores during the "on the green" kneeling ritual right after lunch. The whole freshman class knelt awkwardly in their straight, calf-length skirts, beanied-heads bowed. Clara Belle looked up.

"Do not look me in the eye—you are not worthy—duck that red, Rat head immediately."

As she ducked her head down, the green and white beanie fell off her head to the ground. This was a perpetual problem—the small hat was perched precariously on top of her red frizz and was constantly slipping from one side to the other or just falling off.

"Sorry, Ma'am," said Clara Belle, as she was required to address the upper classman. "Rat Miller requests permission to pick up her beanie and put it back on."

"Permission granted. See that it doesn't happen again at inspection. Now, recite as requested."

Rat Miller recited as requested.

Clara Belle had made the decision early, after her first encounter with this kind of interface, how she would react—she wouldn't. She'd suck it up and just do as she was told. Most all of the girls used this approach. Cravotta was not one of them.

"RAT CRAVOTTA!, are you prepared to salute your superior and say the Class of '61 pledge?" said Meg.

Cravotta just smiled, nodded her head and saluted her own quirky version of the Rat Homage.

"RAT CRAVOTTA! Wipe that silly grin off your face."

"All due respect, Ma'am, but the silly one's all I've got," said Cravotta.

There was a titter amongst the troops.

"Quiet, Rats, there will be no insubordination by encouraging a fellow rat's lack of respect for her superiors. RAT CRAVOTTA! Give me the third verse and chorus of the alma mater."

Cravotta had a voice that was already other-worldly, and when she cranked it up for effect, as she did just then, the result was ear-splitting.

"HAIL ALMA MATER, CROWNED WITH..." she began.

"That will be quite enough, RAT CRAVOTTA!" Meg said, stifling her own laughter and trying to maintain control of the pack of rats who were shaking on their knees.

"Dismissed, Rats!"

The assembly awkwardly rose, straightening their wrinkled and grass-stained skirts and dispersed in all directions across the green.

"Not you, RAT CRAVOTTA!"

Clara Belle watched as Cravotta walked with Meg to the archway. The minute they were out of view of most of the crowd, Meg and Cravotta were laughing together. Meg patted her affectionately on the back and off Cravotta trotted into the dorm, still grinning her silly grin.

At almost every ratting event, something of this sort happened with Cravotta and one of the sophomores—the encounter ended in pretty much the same way. However, one day near the end of Rat Week, the mood changed.

"RAT CRAVOTTA!" said Frances Marie Billingham, a blond priss-pot whom Clara Belle and every other freshman rat avoided. She was from a rich southern aristocratic family and had not had a good experience the year before during her own ratting.

"Yes, Ma'am?" Cravotta grinned.

"Do you have any idea how much trouble you've caused this week?"

"I do my very best, Ma'am."

Snickers from the Rat Troop.

"I will not have your smart mouth insulting me and my fellow superiors."

If Meg or any other sophomores had said this, everyone would be looking forward to what would happen next. But there was an uneasy silence and a sense of apprehension.

"I will try to use my dumb mouth the next time, Ma'am."

Frances Marie Billingham was not amused.

There were no snickers.

These gatherings were public and in sight of anyone passing by, including faculty—there was little chance of anything getting out of hand. Frances Marie Billingham knew better than to carry her attack any further—at least for the moment.

"Rats dismissed," she said, and the rats scattered.

～

There had been rumors toward the end of Rat Week that some dirty tricks were being played on several of the freshmen, which were a bit outside the bounds of lady-like. Personal items were stolen out of rooms, borderline vandalism, and late night visits in which freshmen were forced to get out of bed, undress and stand in the hall until the upperclassman gave them the order to retire.

Clara Belle lived in secluded quarters off the dining hall called Rat Hole. There were seven tiny rooms crammed with two desks, two beds, two dressers and two freshmen. Being assigned to Rat Hole was pure luck and carried with it a certain mystique. Tucked away there, friendships blossomed that lasted for the next four years.

Cravotta lived in Rat Hole at the other end of the hall from Clara Belle. They had not had much contact except this week, as Clara Belle observed her antics with interest and, yes, a bit of admiration. The obvious had not gone unnoticed by Clara Belle that there were certain similarities between them. The differences between them were not as obvious, but no less noticed.

Clara Belle had gone to the Tower Room for a cigarette after studying well into the night. There were only a few girls still up, mostly upperclassmen. One of these was Frances Marie Billingham, who was in deep conversation with another sophomore Clara Belle didn't know. She overheard Cravotta's name several times. When they saw her looking at them, Frances Marie hissed, "What are you looking at Rat-Creep? You should be in bed—you certainly could use some beauty sleep. Get lost!"

Technically, ratting was only supposed to take place during scheduled times and this was not one of them. However, Clara Belle, adhering to her non-confrontational creed said, "Yes, Ma'am," and quickly left the Tower Room and went back to Rat Hole.

Sandra was asleep with all the lights still on—Rat Hole was completely quiet. Clara Belle put on her PJs, grabbed her toothbrush, toothpaste, washrag and soap, turned out the lights and walked down to the communal bathroom at the end of the hall. She peed, washed her face, brushed her teeth and started walking to the door when she heard voices. They were whispering, but loud enough for Clara Belle to recognize the two girls she had just encountered in the Tower Room. She waited as they walked past the bathroom toward the end of the hall. Doors to rooms were never locked and she heard one open and shut. She had a very bad feeling about this and decided to stay put.

About five minutes went by and she heard the door at the end of the hall open and shut again. Again, footsteps past the bathroom door but this time there was no talking, only a muffled sound of some sort. After they had passed, she cracked the door and looked down the hall. There were three girls, the two from the Tower Room and in-between them, with her hands held behind her, a blindfold over her eyes and something stuffed in her mouth, was Cravotta. Shaking, Clara Belle shut the door without a word.

~

"Clara Belle...hey, CB," said Sandra, "you going to breakfast? It's 7:25."

Clara Belle rolled over in her bunk bed and looked at the clock.

"Did my alarm go off?" she groaned.

"Yep, but you were sleeping like the dead—went to take a shower—tried to get a rise out of you but gave up—you all right, you look strange?"

"Did you hear anything last night?" asked Clara Belle.

"Like what? Once I'm asleep I don't hear a thing."

"Never mind."

"I'll save you a seat."

"Don't bother—think I'll skip—not hungry—I'll pick up something over at the Tearoom later."

Clara Belle had not fallen asleep until ...she didn't even know when. She had tried to wait up to hear when Cravotta might return and must have fallen asleep. She didn't remember hearing anything.

She got out of her bed, put on her raincoat and went down to Cravotta's room. There was no one there and everything looked normal—nothing seemed out of order.

Clara Belle decided to look over the railing of the dining hall to see if Cravotta was at breakfast. She wasn't with her roommate, who was eating at the table with other Rat Holers. Clara Belle was beginning to worry, and the sense of guilt she felt was making her physically sick.

She went back to the room, got her bath things and went to take a shower. On the way there she saw Cravotta coming down the hall toward her.

"You all right?" said Clara Belle.

"Why wouldn't I be?" she said sharply.

"I just thought...I mean...last night...I—"

Cravotta shrugged. "Karma rules," she said with a slightly pensive Cravotta grin. She flashed the peace sign with her two fingers and continued down to the dining hall.

Chapter 4

THE SEASON OF HOLY CLOWNS

At an all-women's college such as Southampton, news, good or not-so good, traveled quickly. Clara Belle had waited during the weeks following Rat Week for something to surface about the night Cravotta was taken away by Frances Marie Billingham. Clara Belle understood why those who had perpetrated the deed would not say anything—but why wouldn't Cravotta tell her roommate or somebody about what had happened to her that night? Yet, her odd comment about "karma" struck Clara Belle as more than just a flippant response—perhaps it explained her silence in some way. From that point in time, Clara Belle became a Cravotta watcher.

They had several classes together—English 101 and Western Civilization and an elective, Anthropology 101. Clara Belle had no idea why she had chosen this particular class. Most likely it was because the only other choices were in music and theater, both of which she wished to avoid in keeping with her low-profile strategy.

Cravotta was a brilliant student and dropped any foolishness at the door of the academic world. She wielded her sharp wit, instead, like a saber that cut through any BS a student brought into the class and challenged the professor in duels of ideas and hypotheses.

"Miss Allen," said Dr. Norbett, "we've been exploring the controversies over Margaret Mead's conclusions in interviews with young Samoan women. Would you please give me another anthropologist's view concerning this?"

"I'm sorry, Dr. Norbett," said Mary Allen. "I—"

"Anyone...yes, Miss Cravotta?"

"Most any controversy about her work was because she was a strong, independent woman in a man's world and less about what she had concluded."

"Can you be more specific?"

"Margaret Mead was years ahead of her time. She went to college when most women were at home barefoot and pregnant. When she did get married, she went flying off by herself to a Pacific Island and talked to young girls about having sex with anyone they pleased and enjoying it. Men who challenged her were threatened, plain and simple."

"Thank you, Miss Cravotta. You obviously have read your assignments."

Fortunately for Cravotta, Dr. Norbett was, herself, a strong, independent woman who not only let the frank tirade stand, but appeared to delight in the sexual overtones.

"Miss Miller, what other controversies surrounded Dr. Mead's work and views?"

"Well," said Clara Belle, "she was an early advocate of women's rights, birth control and right to die. That was ten years ago. We're just beginning to make headway in those areas."

"She was married and divorced three times," whined Missie Forsythe. "Seems to me if she'd stayed home more, she might not have so many failed marriages. She—"

"Dr. Mead stated that she didn't consider her marriages failures just because they ended," broke in Cravotta. "She said, and I quote, 'that view is idiotic.' "

Missie was about to shoot back a pithy reply when the chimes in the library rang for end of class.

"All right, ladies," said Dr. Norbett, "I'm assigning a paper—"

Groans.

"That will be quite enough. For this assignment I will ask you to choose a partner with whom you will research and write your paper. The subject will be to cite a common theme among different indigenous cultures and how we can relate that theme to present-day American culture. Remember to partner with someone who shares your interest in the subject you choose. Class dismissed."

As the "ladies" filed out of the room, there were already conversations between some of them about partnerships for the assignment. Clara Belle followed Cravotta back to Rat Hole.

"You decided what you want to write about?" asked Clara Belle.

"Been waiting for a window of opportunity on this one—Sacred Clowns."

Clara Belle's interest was immediately piqued.

"Sacred Clowns?" she said.

"In almost every primitive culture there were special people who did serious clowning—they were an integral part of the tribe—considered to be as important as the shamans and other holy men and women."

Cravotta stopped in her tracks, her dark, marble-eyes locked onto Clara Belle's almond blue ones.

"Well, you want to join me or not? I sense a clown lurking under that refined mask you wear."

"How'd—?"

"Takes one to know one."

~

Working on the research paper provided Cravotta and Clara Belle the opportunity to become friends—becoming Cravotta's friend provided Clara Bell the opportunity to peek out from under her "refined mask" for brief periods of time. She was reluctant to share too much of her early years, while Cravotta spouted like a veritable fountain about her growing up as "a sojourner in a foreign land," as she so biblically put it. There were some similarities, but it was the differences that intrigued Clara Belle.

"At first my parents wanted a little princess, and of course, I was a frog," said Cravotta.

"Did you have someone…I mean, was anyone—?"

"You mean that appreciated me as the amphibian I was?"

"I guess that's what I mean…I had my Aunt Belle who kept harping all the time, 'be yourself, be yourself.' "

"So what happened, huh?"

Cravotta's question hung like a hawk waiting to swoop.

"Got too hard," said Clara Belle.

"Yeah, well, to answer your question, I didn't have an Aunt Belle, but both my parents were pretty cool. My college professor father kept giving me stuff to read from the time I could. Hell, I read Margaret Mead when I was twelve. As a pubescent female, I particularly liked the sexual material. There was one book on the top shelf of his office library called *The Sexual Life of Natives*—I'd climb up to get it whenever no one was home."

"My father is a college professor, too, but he's one who… well…who doesn't quite get me."

"I was lucky, I guess. Not till I went to school did I get how weird my family and I were. You know Margaret Mead was a good friend of Dr. Benjamin Spock—her daughter was probably one of the first children raised by his book. So was I—you know, feed'em when they're hungry, pick'em up when they cry, all that. My mother lived by that book— helped her get over the princess thing early on."

"So it's easy for you?"

"Easy, hell no, never been easy. Look around you at this place—do I fit in here with these southern belles? Who knows why we choose whether to accept ourselves or not? I sure don't. I did have my parents but you had your Aunt Belle and look at you—hiding like a mouse—do you know why?"

Their discussions always seemed to end with a question Clara Belle couldn't or wouldn't answer, which didn't seem to bother Cravotta. The questions did bother Clara Belle and they rolled around in her mind for days and nights afterwards.

There were other pertinent questions evoked by her class in English Literature. She was introduced to writers like Milton, Donne, Byron, Wordsworth, Blake, Frost, who spoke devoutly of spiritual and philosophical themes, but from perspectives and with language unlike anything she had ever encountered in the Brethren Church or at Dayton High, even in Mack's classes. The number of subjects Clara Belle and Cravotta discussed was varied and vast—however, Cravotta wasn't the least interested in dialogues of a spiritual nature.

"Trying to solve the mysteries of the universe is an exercise in futility—God is dead," she stated bluntly.

Aunt Belle and Mack weren't there to bounce ideas off, so having no other close friends with whom to spar, Clara Belle Miller began to explore the mysteries of the universe—by herself. She took long walks down the lake path—by herself. She engaged in stimulating conversation, out loud—with herself. She posed radical philosophical hypotheses and fiercely debated—herself. *Her Self*, she was discovering, was damn good company.

Chapter 5

THE SEASON OF ADVENT

"Hey, CB, want to go to church with me this morning? It's the first Sunday of Advent," said Sandra, coming in from her shower.

"First Sunday of what-vent?" asked Clara Belle.

"Advent—oh, that's right, you've never been to a liturgical church."

"Kindly stop speaking in foreign tongue; I have no idea what you're talking about."

"I'm speaking Episcopalian."

"Oh, Episcopalian—now that's familiar. My cousin's wife is one of those. She's never talked about it, but she's pretty cool about religious stuff."

"OK, first lesson—there are four Sundays in the Season of Advent leading up to Christmas—then we celebrate the Christmas season well into January."

"My Aunt Belle would love that—has a tree up most of the year and she's Methodist."

"So you've really never been in an Episcopal church?"

"Nope, I'm a liturgical virgin."

"Good a time as any to de-flower you, religiously speaking," laughed Sandra, "Advent is fun—builds up the excitement—you ought to see what we do with Lent and Easter."

"Whoa—one season at a time—OK, I'll go."

"Better get ready, the van picks us up at 10:30 for the 11:00 o'clock Euchari....sorry, service."

"This better be worth my getting up. It's been a blessing from God not having parents dragging me out of bed on Sunday."

"No promises. I'll warn you, it's a little like Catholic—won't freak you out, will it?"

"My Granddaddy Miller would have a cow," Clara Belle laughed, "but I'll never tell."

They got dressed and fixed a cup of instant coffee. They divided the last of the Krispy Kreme donuts from the box they had bought last week from one of the clubs on campus, then went downstairs to the dorm entrance to wait for the van. There were five other girls waiting, looking very sleepy, but choosing, as Sandra was, to go to church even when they didn't have to.

The church van arrived and the girls climbed in—it drove into the city of Greensboro and pulled up to an imposing stone building with massive, bright red wooden doors—not in the least like Garber's Church.

"Do I do anything different?" asked Clara Belle as they walked toward the entrance.

"Probably everything, but just watch me. Actually, you can just sit and stand when the congregation does—you don't have to kneel," said Sandra.

"Kneel—did you say kneel? The only person I ever saw kneel in the Brethren Church was Herman Kunz, a lay preacher who was asked to give the prayer once in awhile—he'd use it as an opportunity for a sermon on his knees. Like that kind of 'on your knees' kneel?"

"Like on your...there are benches...never mind, just relax, follow my lead."

As Clara Belle took a bulletin and entered the door, she was totally unprepared for the effect the building itself would have on her. Her mouth dropped open as the breath seemed to be sucked from her lungs. The church was cold but her total body shiver was not from the temperature.

The vaulted ceiling seemed to go on forever, and the sun shining through the stained glass windows that lined both sides of the sanctuary gave it an otherworldly glow. The organ was playing a triumphant prelude but Clara Belle could see no organ, no organist. Not until she turned around halfway down the center aisle to their pew did she see a large loft at the very back of the church where a man sat on a long bench at a console with three sets of keys and all manner of knobs on either side. In front of him were hundreds of pipes of every size from a very large factory chimney to a tiny kitchen pipe.

"Your mouth is hanging," whispered Sandra as they sat down.

Sandra immediately reached toward the bottom of the pew in front of them and pulled down a little bench covered with a red cushion. Clara Belle watched as Sandra knelt, bowed her head and closed her eyes for a few moments and then returned to the pew.

The organ paused after the prelude ended and then began what was apparently an introduction to the first hymn—everyone in the congregation stood. Down the aisle marched a young man wearing a black robe overlaid with a white one. He was carrying a large brass cross mounted on a wooden pole. As he passed each pew, heads, and sometimes bodies, bent in silent homage. The young man was followed by other teenaged boys carrying tall, lit, tapered candles placed in brass candleholders.

Then came the choir, two by two, dressed the same as the cross and candle-bearers, singing a hymn Clara Belle had never heard, but touching her as somehow familiar. She glanced at her hymnal. "O Come, O Come Emanuel" was being sung in unison and sounded like monks in a monastery. The four-part harmony of familiar hymns in the Brethren hymnal with the simple accompaniment of a small upright piano in tiny Garber's Church was a world away from this—and yet she felt strangely at home.

The procession ended with several elaborately robed ministers. When the two-by-two choir members reached the front pew, they bowed, split, one going right, one left, and continued along the side aisles, up steps at the rear of the church to join the organist in the loft. The candle and crossbearers and the ministers walked up to the magnificent altar.

During the remainder of the service, Clara Belle sat absorbed in an entirely new church experience. The chanting, the prayers from the prayer book, the continuous kneeling, standing, sitting, standing, kneeling, sitting, instead of confusing or annoying her, exhilarated and moved her. She didn't know a single hymn or chant that was sung; yet she sang as if she had known them always. The only thing familiar was the scripture. The reader rose and walked to the pulpit and began, "A reading from Isaiah: 'then a shoot shall grow from the stock of Jesse and a branch shall spring from its roots—' "

Clara Belle said each word silently with the reader until he ended saying, "The Word of the Lord."

"Thanks be to God," said the congregation.

As soon as she got back to the dorm, she ran to the phone and dialed the number. The phone rang and rang. She was about to hang up when a voice said, "Hello."

"Melinda," said Clara Belle, "why didn't you tell me?"

Chapter 6

THE COMMUNICATION GAP

Aunt Belle's incommunicado with her favorite niece during that first semester of college was intentional—difficult, but necessary. After their last parlor talk she realized that the time had come to let Clara Belle find her own way back to herself. She'd done and said everything that needed doing and saying—all she could do now was pray that at least some of her experience and advice might be useful.

Clara Belle had not come home for Thanksgiving or any other time, for that matter. She called her father occasionally to report her grades, her mother to report some news of what she was doing. She had written one letter to Aunt Belle about halfway through the semester. The good news was that she had made a friend with a strange name Aunt Belle couldn't remember—Carlotta or something. That's where she had gone Thanksgiving. They lived in the same dorm and had several classes together. The high point of this friendship seemed to have been a paper they wrote on something called "Sacred Clowns," whatever they were. The subject apparently had fascinated Clara Belle and Aunt Belle could only hope that this was a good sign. Hell, any kind of clown was a good sign, even a damned sacred one.

The phone rang.

"Hello," she said.

The voice at the other end of the line was vaguely familiar.

"Hello, Mrs. Lincoln, this is Mack McDonald from Dayton High—I was Clara Belle's teacher. Is she coming home for Christmas?"

"Yes, Mr. McDonald, she is."

" Do you know when?" he asked.

"I think around the eighteenth—not sure."

"I'd like to get in touch with her before—do you have her address at school?"

"Don't know it right off—let me get it."

She put down the phone and went to find her address book. When she finally found it in a pile of cookbooks, she picked it up carefully. She'd had this one for at least twenty-five years and several pages fluttered to the floor.

"Damn," she said, picking them up and stuffing them back where she hoped they belonged. She went back to the phone.

"Sorry it took so long, now let me see, M's , M's - shit… sorry, half these people are dead—just don't have the heart to scratch them out—makes it so permanent."

She finally found the scrawled note under "C" for Clara Belle.

"OK, here it is… P. O. Box 757, Southampton College, Greensboro, North Carolina. That all you need?"

"Mrs. Lincoln, do you think…I mean…is it appropriate?"

"Appropriate—sure, why not? She's a big college girl now."

"I was hoping you'd say that—good to talk to you."

"Good to talk to you, too."

She hung up the phone and smiled.

"YES!" she said.

∼

Clara Belle was not looking forward to Christmas vacation, but she had little choice in the matter. After the major scene with her parents when she told them she was going to northern Virginia with Cravotta over the short Thanksgiving break, they'd only agreed if she promised to come home for the two-week Christmas vacation.

The weekend at Cravotta's had been a bit strange and a little challenging for her. Clara Belle had never been around anyone her age that behaved exactly the same with her parents as she did with her peers. That was the strange part; the challenging part for her was which Clara Belle would be their guest? The precarious balancing game she was playing between the Clara Belle who fit in with the college scene and the Clara Belle who was Cravotta's friend went out of whack when she was interacting with adults who were eccentric and brilliant, and who accepted their equally eccentric and brilliant daughter just as she was. She had no idea who to be. She mentioned this to Cravotta when they got back.

"When you find yourself not thinking about who you are, that's when you are," said Cravotta.

"Who says you're not a philosopher?"

"I'm a realist."

The week before the Christmas break, she went to her mailbox. She usually had a letter from her mother—her father wrote after each grading period, commenting on how well she had done, or how she could do better. Today, there was a letter in a messy handwriting she didn't recognize. The initials MM were at the top of the return address, which was Dayton, Virginia. She quickly opened the envelope.

"Hello, Clara Belle,

How are things going there in the sunny south?"

She looked down at the signature at the bottom "Mack, alias Mr. McDonald."

"Hey," said Sandra, who had just claimed her mail, "you look as red as your hair—what's up?"

"I just got a letter from somebody I didn't expect."

"Well, you'd better finish reading it—looks like it might make your day."

"Oh, it's nothing, he was just my teacher in high school."

"One of those 'To Sir With Love,' scenarios?"

"N-Not...he's j-just—" she began.

Sandra laughed, "You don't lie very well."

Clara Belle left the mailroom and walked down by the lake to finish the letter. She was embarrassed and mystified by her reaction—God, she had even started stuttering again. What the hell was that all about?

She sat down on one of the cement benches by the lake and read the letter.

Hello, Clara Belle,

How are things going there in the sunny south? Things here in the metropolis of Dayton are about the same, and Dayton High continues on its uphill path to educational excellence for future farmers and homemakers.

Your Aunt Belle (she gave me your address) tells me you're coming home for Christmas, and I was hoping we might get together to talk about what you are doing down there. I hear there are some things being planned in the area to raise awareness about those kids in Little Rock who integrated Central High School last year. They've come up with a new kind of protest called a sit-in at some all-white businesses. Thought you might already be involved.

If it's all right, I'll give you a call when you get here. Hope everything is going well. I miss having you around.

Sincerely,

Mack, alias Mr. McDonald

Chapter 7

THE SEXUAL RESOLUTION

"So, which is it? You afraid he has the hots for you or that you have the hots for him?"

They were sitting on the beds in Cravotta's room. Her roommate had gone home for the weekend.

Clara Belle ducked her head and again felt her face flush.

"Good God, Clara Belle, are we having our first sex talk here?"

"Come on, CRAVOTTA!, I grew up on a farm—I saw cows and sheep do it before I was five."

"Not the same; that's like me reading about Samoan girls and sexual life of the natives, not the same at all. Real sex is what we're talking here—humans with other humans."

"So, CRAVOTTA! Exactly how many times have you done it with a real person, huh?"

Cravotta gave her a sheepish grin. "Just once…with a boy in my neighborhood when I was fifteen—lasted about five minutes, including foreplay. But still, I've messed around in the back seat of a Chevy enough to recognize the feelings when I have them—you?"

"I guess…not really…didn't think about it much. My first cousin Jorda—"

"Whoa, that sounds a bit like ince—"

"No…no…not like that at all. He and I were just close… kind of special in a way. He was really my best…my only friend for a long time until…well, a long time. Kind of took care of me—protected me from other kids giving me too rough a time early on."

"Ever have a real boyfriend?"

"Never thought of myself as a candidate for anybody's girlfriend and I guess nobody else did either. I could talk to boys real easy because of Jordan, and I told dirty jokes, which made them like me in that way. But no, I guess I never had a boyfriend like you're talking about."

"Ever been kissed, with tongue—without tongue?"

Clara Belle made a face.

"I met this boy named Marlin at all-state band when I was a freshman in high school...hmm, guess he did look a little like an ape, but was nice—we wrote for a while—asked me to his prom but my parents wouldn't let me go. Sort of hoped that might be the occasion for my first kiss—didn't happen."

"OK, so we've established that you know all about the mechanics, you have the desire for the opposite sex, so you're not a lesbian. So what's your problem with the possibility that the Big Mack-ster might want more than a serious talk about the Civil Rights Movement?"

"He's too old—"

"Didn't you say he was twenty-four? You're what, nineteen? That's five year's difference. Don't buy that—keep digging."

Clara Belle got up from the bed and started pacing.

"What's really bugging you about this? What about him makes you afraid to be more than student-teacher. Talk to me, CB."

"I bet Aunt Belle put him up—"

"Evasion alert—evasion alert!!"

Clara Belle walked to the door, opened it, then slammed it shut and turned around abruptly.

"The last thing he said to me before I left was a threat."

"What do you mean a threat?"

"He said I damn well better do more than just try to survive."

"BINGO!!"

"I need a cigarette," said Clara Belle.

"Now we're talking."

Chapter 8

THE HOME FIRE'S BURNING

~Melinda~

"Let's have Clara Belle over for dinner and conversation," I said. "She'll like coming back to the little house."

"She probably doesn't even know where her parents have moved—hasn't been home since she left for college. I haven't even had a postcard from her. Have you?" said Jordan.

"I'm sure she keeps in touch with them. You sound like you're pouting. Good grief, Jordan, you ignored her for years, your little make-up session can't wipe that all away in one fell swoop."

"Am not pouting, I just wish—"

Clara Belle hadn't written to me either. After we had our little talk up at Granddaddy Miller's and she was in the wedding before she left, I had hoped we might become good friends, but that didn't happen. Not that there had been a lot of time, but still. She had called about going to the Episcopal Church. She was so excited that Sunday and we talked for a while about my experience with the church. I thought we might use that common interest to build more of a relationship but she never called again. I didn't tell Jordan—he would have been hurt.

The little house had always been a "start-up" house for newlyweds in the Miller family. Jordan decided to get his Master's at Madison College where Uncle Ben Jr. taught—his uncle and Aunt Mary Faith decided to move into town to be closer to his work. I loved the quaint little house and what it brought out in Jordan. He was quite often reminded of a Clara Belle story, which I loved to hear. I had high hopes that Christmas would be a time for both Jordan and me to build some adult-style relationship with his cousin.

~Mary Faith~

Even though Mary Faith understood why Clara Belle didn't keep in touch as much as she'd like, and was even a little pleased about her having a friend that she felt close enough to go home with at Thanksgiving, she just plain missed her only daughter. They had shared so much for eighteen years and this was just hard, that's all.

When Ben Jr. had decided to move to a larger house in Harrisonburg, she had reluctantly left the farm. Even though he pretended this was for Melinda and Jordan's benefit, she knew his real motives and wasn't particularly proud of them. He had always been embarrassed by his farm origins and wanted to be nearer the academic world where he aspired to fit in.

"The president's Christmas reception is a must, Mary Faith—you simply have to go. And I'm sure that it would be appropriate to invite Clara Belle while she's home and I would expect her to go."

"Ben, she could care less about a president's reception— she's not going to want—"

"Mary Faith, she'll want to go to graduate school—"

"She's a freshman, Ben!"

"One just can't start making connections too early. Look at Jordan; he's already planning to teach at Madison when he's finished his Master's."

"Is that his plan or yours?"

Ben ignored her insinuation.

"Just give her some space, will you?" said Mary Faith.

"Space…she's had space…she hasn't come home since August. It's time for her to start planning for her future."

"I just want her home—just want her here."

"Mrs. Lincoln, this is Mack McDonald again, I'd—"

"Belle, call me Belle for Pete's sake."

"All right, Mrs. Belle."

He could feel her frustration right through the phone line.

"How about Aunt Belle, then?" she said.

"I think I can do that—I've heard it enough from Clara Belle, which is why I called."

"Figured," said Aunt Belle.

"I've written her; did she tell you?"

"Not a word."

"I was wondering if I could... you could give me some idea—"

"Glad to give you any help you need—not that I have any clue to what that might be."

"I'm not sure I know either. Could I come to your house next week when I get out of school, before she gets here?"

"How about next Thursday afternoon?"

"Sounds good—about 4:00 OK?"

"Fine—you know where we are?"

"Hinton, right?"

"Next to the water tower with the big 'H'—that's for Henry, you know."

Clara Belle had not answered the letter he had written and he was disappointed. She had been such a breath of fresh air for him her junior and senior years at Dayton High. Their conversations on social issues and other important topics that seemed to interest no one else in the area had kept him motivated to continue his passions. And there was the play, when she had finally shown some of that spirit she held so tightly in check—he had felt a part of bringing that out in her. For a teacher, what could possibly be more rewarding? And she'd never even had a crush on him like some of the other girls there.

The next week he arrived at Aunt Belle's, not at all sure of his motives.

"Hello, Mrs....Sorry, Aunt Belle."

"Hello, Mack—want some coffee, tea, a left-over Jesse's dog with chili?"

"Think I'll pass, thanks."

"Come on back, seems like the parlor suits this occasion."

"Heard about that parlor. Is the tree up yet?"

"Ta-Dah," she said as they walked into the parlor. "Sit!"

He sat down on one of the velvet parlor chairs and looked around the room where Clara Belle had spent so many hours soaking up encouragement and wisdom from this unique woman.

"Is that the tin box she told me about?" he asked, looking at the roll-top desk.

"Surprised she even told you—never seemed impressed—maybe someday."

He paused, not knowing how to begin.

"Aunt Belle, I wrote her—she didn't write back or call—any idea why?"

"Don't take it personal—none of us has heard much and you know she didn't come home at Thanksgiving."

"You think she's all right?"

"I have a good feeling about what she's doing—getting away—experimenting with herself. Even wrote a paper on something called Sacred Clowns, whatever the hell they are—can you beat that?"

"That's encouraging. Anything else—involved in any civil rights activities?"

"Not that I know of—I think she's keeping a low profile."

He cleared his throat.

"I really have missed having her around."

Aunt Belle's eyes narrowed at him and she said sternly, "Your intentions are honorable, aren't they?"

"Of course, Mrs. Lincoln...I would ne—"

She threw back her blond head and her dangly earrings jangled, "Just jerking you around, Mr. McDonald. I'm certain you have sense enough to go slow with her—even if your intentions go deeper than perhaps even you know. You have my blessing, for what that's worth."

"It's worth more than you know—thanks, Aunt Belle."

Chapter 9

THE HOME-BE-COMING

Clara Belle was packing the last of her things for the visit home.

Cravotta was sitting on Sandra's bed, knitting.

"I'm not coming back next semester, Clara Belle."

"CRAVOTTA! You can't mean that—you can't do that to me—where are you going? Damn…Why?…I mean, I know why…but why so soon?"

"Life's too short and this has been the longest four months of my life—I gotta get out of this place—it's smothering me. Other than you, I can't relate to one thing here."

"Was it what happened Rat Week?" she asked cautiously. They had never talked about that night.

Cravotta's faced darkened.

"What happened, happened—only a small blip on the radar of this decision. I let that one go the day after."

"What're you going to do?"

"After Christmas vacation and exams, I'm going home until I decide what to do next."

"You going to another college?"

"Not sure—lots going on in the world out there—may take time for adventures of some kind or another."

"So you'll be here when we get back from Christmas break, right?"

"I want to get the credits I've earned in case I need them—yeah, I'll be back."

"Well, I'll see you then—thanks for everything."

"Good luck being back in the cradle again."

"What the hell is that supposed to mean?"

"You know damn well—and Clara Belle—"

"What?"

"Give the Big Mack a little squeeze from Cravotta."

"Screw you."

"On your mind, huh?"

~

The bus ride home had taken forever, and the closer she came, the more nervous she became. And it wasn't just seeing Mr. McDonald, either; she wasn't looking forward to this homecoming with anyone—she hadn't seen them for four months and that hadn't been half bad.

The bus pulled up to the Harrisonburg station. She looked out the window and saw her father waiting. She was relieved, in a way. This relationship was predictable—it hadn't changed. She had learned to live with what her father expected from her and knew exactly how to react.

"Hello, Clara Belle, it's good to see you after all this time," he said, as she stepped off the bus.

"Hello, Daddy, good to see you, too…where's Mom?"

"She wanted to get things ready for you at the new house. She's been working on your room. She's real excited about you coming home—been a long time."

"You said that already."

"Well, Clara Belle, it has…you know how your mother is—"

"Dad, I'm here now, can we leave it at that?"

"Can see you haven't changed much."

"Neither have you."

They got her bags and went to the car.

"You ready for exams? Guess you'll have to hit the books all during your break."

"I have two term papers to do—one for anthropology and one for English. I wish we were on a system where we had exams before Christmas like some schools—really messes up a vacation."

"Madison does it that way—makes it easier on the students, harder on us—we have the papers to grade over the break."

"How do you like living in the big city?" Clara Belle asked.

"I like being close to the college—gives me a chance to hobnob with the faculty, which is important for both of us."

"Both of who—?"

"This is it—Casa Miller—pretty up-scale, huh?"

Clara Belle looked at the large brick house that sat on a tree-lined street of old faculty houses near the college.

"Nice," she said, just as her mother ran out the front door toward her. Her arms were stretched out in a welcoming hug and Clara Belle received the welcome with an unexpected clutch in her chest.

"Clara Belle, my baby, Clara Belle, I'm so glad you're home."

"You've already had a bunch of phone calls," her mother said. "Melinda called and she and Jordan want to have you over for a meal at the little house—Aunt Belle, of course, and you know what, that nice Mr. McDonald, you remember from Dayton, called and left his number for you to call when you got here—now wasn't that nice?"

Her mother rattled on and on and Clara Belle let her, because it occurred to her suddenly how hard her own absence must have been for this woman who had stood by her all these years.

"Mom, I'm sorry I didn't—"

"Clara Belle, I understand, you needed to do that—but you're home now and you won't ever have to prove anything to yourself anymore. Let's just enjoy this."

∼

Aunt Belle would be the next homecoming visit on her list. The last time they talked had been the morning after her clown dream. Clara Belle had left on fairly good terms after telling her aunt exactly where she stood about college. She had received one letter from Aunt Belle and in that letter she hadn't preached or lectured, so maybe this wouldn't be too painful.

Clara Belle pulled up to the old house in her mother's blue and white Chevrolet sedan. Mary Faith had insisted that Clara Belle use it for the two weeks she was home. It was great to have wheels again—freshmen were not allowed to have cars until second semester and Clara Belle was hoping she could talk her parents into letting her take this car back—the bus ride was endless with all the stopping at every one-horse town.

"Hey, turd-head, want to go play doctor in the wash house?" said Hank Jr., coming out the back door.

"What about a snipe hunt, fart-brain?" she countered.

He gave her a perfunctory pat on the shoulder and went toward Uncle Henry's office. "Gotta go to work—the boss is a slave driver."

Aunt Belle was standing on the porch with the door open, waiting.

"Well, you comin' in or what?"

"Hi, Aunt Belle, good to see you."

"It is…yep, it is."

Without even thinking, Clara Belle walked toward the parlor—Aunt Belle followed.

They sat down opposite each other.

Clara Belle waited—Aunt Belle waited.

"Nice tree," said Clara Belle.

"It's fake," said Aunt Belle.

"That way you won't have to take it down at all."

"My thought exactly."

Aunt Belle waited—Clara Belle waited.

"Sacred clowns," said Aunt Belle.

"What about them?"

"What the hell are they?"

"I'll let you read my paper—got an A."

"Good for you."

"You mad at me for not writing much, or calling?"

"Nope."

"Everybody else is."

"Their problem."

"Aunt Belle, why is this so weird with us today?"

"Weird? Really? Hadn't noticed."

Aunt Belle lifted up her hip and let a loud fart.

Both of them dissolved into laughter.

Chapter 10

THE LITTLE HOUSE —
SECOND GENERATION

She spent the next few days around the new house studying and going to the Madison Library to research for her term papers. This, of course, pleased her father and gave them a chance to talk. Unfortunately for Clara Belle, all he wanted to talk about was what was she going to major in and where was she going to graduate school.

She had accepted Melinda and Jordan's invitation for dinner on Friday night before Christmas at the little house. She decided this would also be a good time for a little visit with Granddaddy Miller. He was living up at the home-place alone and was doing very well at eighty-five. He still walked the farm with his cane, singing to himself and counting Angus.

She drove up the lane, past Jordan's home place, the little house, the cemetery and the other farm buildings—nothing had changed. As she got out of the car, she looked up at the old barn expecting Moses to yell "Help" and was tempted to go up and have a swing on the rope. She looked at her watch—another time.

When she went in the house, Granddaddy Miller was, as usual, lying on the couch in the living room. At first he was confused about who she was, but as soon as she started talking, he said, "So, kleine clown, have you a joke for your old Grandfatter?"

"The ones I learn at a girl's college you wouldn't think were very funny."

"College, yet—where the time goes?"

He closed his eyes and she thought he was going to sleep. They popped open and he said, "Home for the Miller Christmas, yah?"

"Yah," she said. "Anybody having a Miller Christmas breakfast?"

"The aunts, they try something new this year. No breaking of the fast, something in evening, after Christmas. Ask Belle—it will be by Hinton, I'm thinking."

"I'll sure miss all that food and presents."

"You are missing, also, the envelopes on the tree, yet?" he chuckled.

"My daddy, Mr. Economics Professor, invested almost all of that money and now I have a pretty good stash. It became mine when I turned eighteen—haven't touched it so far."

"Smart girl—saving for a rainy day is good business."

"Granddaddy Miller, you remember that old tin box? You told Jordan and me about it being a treasure."

"Yah, a treasure it is."

"Aunt Belle says it's a treasure, too—as a little girl I didn't understand how a bunch of old yellow papers could be a treasure—I still don't."

"You read the papers, yah?"

"Uh…no."

"Well then." He closed his eyes and she knew their visit was over.

She pulled into the driveway at the little house behind a beat-up VW van. Jordan and Melinda came out on the front porch—now she was home.

Melinda ran to her and gave her a big hug. Jordan hung back for a moment, then joined them in an awkward group hug, surprising all three of them.

"Welcome home, cousin," he said. "It's about time."

"Jordan!" Melinda scolded.

"Come on in—see what we've done with the place," he said, ignoring his wife's dirty look.

"Wow," Clara Belle said, looking around at the newly wed cottage decor.

"Amazing what a couple of cans of Sherwin-Williams and hand-me-down furniture can do," said Melinda.

"Looks great, Jor...Doo-Dah," said Clara Belle, and everyone relaxed.

Over dinner in the tiny dining room, Clara Belle told them about her college semester and the new couple talked about Jordan's school and Melinda's work. Melinda was intrigued by the Cravotta stories. Jordan quizzed her on what subjects she was taking and exactly how she planned to use her education.

"For pity's sake, Doo-Dah, you sound like Daddy. I have no clue what my major will be—we don't have to declare until the end of the freshman year. I've got plenty of time."

"But why waste second semester on classes that you won't need for your degree?"

"What about drama—you doing any plays or anything?" said Melinda.

"No, haven't had a lot of time for that."

"How about comparative religion classes—as I remember, you had a pretty good grasp of that subject early on, much to my Aunt Deputy Do-Good's dismay."

"Am pretty much sticking to a straight liberal arts curriculum—nothing too far out other than going to the Episcopal church."

"How disappointing," said Melinda.

"How refreshing," said Jordan. "What's that about the Epis—"

The phone rang in the kitchen.

Melinda got up from the table and went into the kitchen to answer it.

"Clara Belle, it's for you," she said.

"For me? Who is it, Mom, Aunt Belle?"

"No, it's a man—don't recognize his voice."

She walked to the kitchen and picked up the phone.

"Hello," she said.

"Hello, Clara Belle, it's Mack McDonald. I called your house and your mother gave me this number—I hope you don't mind."

Her stomach lurched and she felt a stab of guilt—her mother had told her the first day that he'd left his number—she hadn't called him back.

"No, it's fine, how are you?"

"I'm just fine. Hey, listen, I was wondering if you had a little time before you go back to school to get together?"

She paused, her heart racing.

"Just a minute," she said, putting her hand over the receiver. "Melinda, Doo-Dah, it's Mr. McDonald—would it be OK if he came over here for a little while?"

"Sure, we'd be happy to entertain your boyfriend," Melinda laughed.

"Shush, he's not—"

"Mr. McDonald?"

"Please call me Mack."

"OK, Ma...can't do...sorry...Doing anything now?" she asked.

"Not really."

"Why don't you come over here for a while—we're just getting ready to have dessert."

"Well...I guess...sure...why not? See you in fifteen minutes."

"OK then, bye."

She hung up the phone and couldn't stop shaking.

"Isn't that the teacher you had at Dayton—the one that got you in that play?" asked Melinda.

"Yes."

"Well, what's going on?"

"Nothing...I'm not sure, to tell you the truth—but I figure there's safety in numbers."

"I think it's great," said Melinda. "You were like the Clara Belle I saw growing up when you were with him at the graduation party we had."

"On second thought, maybe it's not such a good idea after all," said Jordan.

"Oh, Jordan, don't be such a fart-head-stick-in-the mud," said Melinda.

"Whoa, Melinda, I think I'm going to like having you in the clan."

"Speaking of family, you're going to be an....aunt?...no that's not right, a cousin-in-law?...whatever, I don't know... Jordan and I are expecting."

"No sh...no kidding. That was quick. I thought you wanted to keep teaching awhile."

"Never did want to be a career woman. I'd actually work longer, just because we need the money, but Rockingham County School Board has a rule, if you're showing, you can't teach—a little absurd since all the kids I teach live on farms and watch the reproductive process unfold in living color every day. The idea that humans might be up to the same thing threatens the adults in the system, I guess."

"Congratulations—when?"

"She probably shouldn't have told you yet—it's early— you never know what might...not until July," said Jordan.

"Jordan, you are such a poop," said Melinda.

Car lights came around the corner of the chicken house and pulled up in the drive.

Clara Belle watched out the front window as Mack got out of the car. The light from the garage shone on him as he walked slowly around Jordan's van. He stopped several times, looking in the windows, smiled and slapped his leg, patted the roof, then started toward the porch.

Clara Belle waited until he knocked before she walked toward the door. She waited a few beats, took a deep breath and opened the door, wondering how she should greet him.

He bounded in like a large puppy, grabbed her in a bear hug and swung her around. Oddly enough, this seemed the most natural thing and then she remembered—he had done the same thing right after Brother Goose—like a fatherly coach with his players after a basketball game—the most appropriate of gestures.

"Come right in, Mack, welcome to the Glick's little house," said Melinda, grinning from ear to ear.

Jordan stuck out his hand.

"Nice to have you, Mr. McDonald."

"Mack...please call me Mack," he said, giving Clara Belle a fake scowl.

"Whose are the bitch'n wheels out there?" asked Mack. "Always wanted one of those."

"I get the credit for that one," said Melinda. "Best deal we've made so far—except, of course, this free house. It's a 1950s vintage, but in good condition and runs like a dream. Cozy accommodations in the rear, too," she grinned and patted her stomach.

Clara Belle blushed and Jordan glared at his wife as she grabbed Mack's arm and led him to the dining room.

"I've got Sarah Lee pound cake, with or without chocolate ice cream—any takers?"

"Sounds good to me—with, please," said Mack.

"Just coffee for me—I ate too much dinner," said Clara Belle.

"With," said Jordan, "and coffee, please—Mack?"

"Black, thanks."

They settled in around the table as Melinda and Clara Belle served the dessert and coffee. The conversation was casual and easy, and Clara Belle relaxed and noted how comfortable Mack seemed around Melinda and Jordan— maybe because they were about the same age. It suddenly struck her, "he isn't really that old."

Clara Belle observed Mr. Mack McDonald in a new way that evening. She listened as he discussed politics and education with Jordan, with whom he mostly disagreed—about social issues, religion and the arts with Melinda, with whom he mostly agreed. His blue eyes sparkled with intensity and his hands were always in motion to punctuate each point he wanted to drive home—and there were many. She joined in the discussion now and again when she had her own point to make but remained somewhat detached, watching, watching and feeling…feeling what?

"Anybody want some schnapps?" asked Melinda. "We Episcopalians, though traditionally English, have adopted this fine German tradition—although Dunkard Granddaddy Miller would hardly approve."

"Count me in," said Mack. "We Irish are also very willing to give other cultures a try—especially when it comes to booze."

"Melinda, do you think—" said Jordan.

"Don't worry, I'm not. Something tells me this is not the time. Clara Belle, what about you?"

"I've never had a drink in my life," she said.

"Away at college for a semester—you're kidding?" said Mack.

Clara Belle stood up, raised her right hand in the air and recited, "According to the little white handbook, 'It is not becoming of a Southampton lady to consume alcohol on campus.' " She sat down. "And, we never get off campus."

"Pity," said Melinda.

"Don't like the stuff myself—I'll have a beer," said Jordan.

"Clara Belle?" said Melinda.

"What the hell—worth a try—I'm in safe company, yes?" She shot a look at Mack.

"Harmless," he said, placing his hand over his heart.

Melinda got the drinks. She set tiny glasses of the clear liquid in front of Mack and Clara Belle, a bottle of beer for Jordan and a Coke for her.

"Proust," said Mack as he took a big gulp.

"Cheers," said Clara Belle, taking a swallow and immediately started choking.

"That is awful stuff," she said. "Tastes like rubbing alcohol."

"Take it a little slower—you need to build up an immunity to it—like the plague."

The time slipped away, as did the schnapps, until Melinda started yawning.

"I'm pooped," she said. "Guess it's this 'with child' thing going on. You guys excuse me."

Mack looked at his watch.

"Holy Cow, it's 1:30—time for me to be gone. Thanks, Jordan, Melinda—great evening, good company, good schnapps, grown-up conversation. A real luxury for a high school teacher."

Clara Belle stood up, feeling a little woozy, "Me too," she said. "The parents will be wondering. Thanks you two—it's been the best."

She steadied herself on the back of a chair.

"Clara Belle, why don't you stay over—I don't think you should drive," said Jordan.

"Good idea," said Melinda. "We have a great couch right here."

"I agree," said Mack. "Don't want to have you running some Mennonite off the road in the middle of the night."

"They don't stay up this late," said Clara Belle.

"Some of those young bucks do—I've seen them carousing on their bikes. Oh, what the folks would say. Night, Jordan, Melinda, thanks again."

"Anytime," said Melinda, yawning and wandering down the hall.

"Goodnight," said Jordan. "Clara Belle, Mack, good to see you both again."

Mack walked to the door and Clara Belle unthinkingly followed him out to the car.

"I could drive you home," said Mack.

"No, thanks, I'll just stay here—for old time's sake."
She leaned up against his car.
"Could we do something again…before you go back…
when do you go back?" Mack said.
"January 4th—we have exams two weeks after…sure."
"Sure, what?"
"Sure, let's…you know…do something."
"Call you tomorrow," he said.
"OK, sure, call me tomorrow."
"Well, goodnight, Clara Belle, really great to see you."
"Same here," she said pausing a moment.
Mack paused a moment, too, then turned to his car.
"Tomorrow, then," he said, opening the door.
She started toward the house.
CRAVOTTA! You're so damn smart.

Chapter 11

THE MILLER CHRISTMAS—PRESENT

"Aunt Belle, what's the deal on the Miller Christmas this year? Granddaddy Miller says you're having it and it's at night after Christmas. Sounds a little weird to me," said Clara Belle into the phone.

"Not crazy about the idea myself, but with families living all over the place now, Clara and Lillian and some of the others thought they'd want to have Christmas morning at their own houses—so there you go."

"You fixing supper for everybody—what are we eating?"

"Everybody brings finger food of some kind. I'll provide paper plates, drinks and whatever else we need. Starts at 5 o'clock and people can stay as long as they want."

"OK then," said Clara Belle, pausing.

"We done?" asked Aunt Belle.

"You remember my English teacher at Dayton High—the one that got me to do the play?"

"Sure, that nice Mr. McDonald."

"Did you put him up to writing me at school?"

"Course not, he called me for your address."

"Well, I saw him last week at Melinda and Jordan's and we've…we've been …we've spent some time doing…stuff this week. You think it would be all right if I asked him to the Christmas thing on the 29th?"

"Think he can handle the Miller clan?"

"Says he's from a big family in Colorado—I guess so."

"If you want to bring a bottle of something more than Coke, we're hiding a cooler from Granddaddy on the side porch."

"I'll tell Mack—I'll pass. I can still feel the burn of that damn schnapps Melinda talked me into last week."

"Bring him on," said Aunt Belle.

"OK then, we'll see you awhile after things get started."

"Sneaking in under the radar, huh?"

"Something like that—Bye, Aunt Belle. Are you sure you didn't...I mean...it was his idea, right?"

"Scout's honor."

"You were in the 4-H Club."

"Same thing." And she hung up.

~

Mary Faith had watched Clara Belle closely ever since she came home from Jordan and Melinda's dinner last week. Clara Belle hadn't even bothered to call about sleeping over and Mary Faith worried when she woke up at 2:00 AM and the car wasn't back. She had become accustomed to not worrying after Clara Belle went off to college—that was easy. Her coming home as an adult, keeping her own hours—this was hard. When Clara Belle had come home the next morning, she mumbled something and went right to her room and slept until noon.

Then there was this thing with Mr. McDonald, who Clara Belle was now calling "Mack."

"They're spending an awful lot of time together, don't you think, Ben?" she said.

"Yes, yes, they are—but I'm very pleased that he's helping her with her term papers and reviewing for exams—I think she was getting a little tired of me."

"But they went to a concert the other night at the Lutheran Church and they come in really late—I mean, is this man a tutor or a suitor?"

"He is a bit older than she."

"That doesn't bother me—he's just a little older than Jordan. But Ben, she's never had a boyfriend that we know of. She goes to an all-girl college—had no experience with men. I don't know—you think I ought to talk to her?"

"If it'll make you feel better—you want I should talk to him?"

"Heavens, no, she'd be mortified. She'll be going back to school in less than a week—not much time for anything to go that wrong, I guess. She's invited him to Belle's tonight, you know."

"What...she ha...why would she do that? We only brought somebody to a Miller get-together if we were engaged or getting ready to. Maybe there's more to worry about than I thought. I'll take him aside tonight—get a feel for what's going on."

"Ben, no, please—not tonight. Let's just leave it alone for now."

~

In the early days of Jordan and Clara Belle, the trip to Aunt Belle's took forever. Tonight, the time was going much too quickly. What had she been thinking, inviting Mack to the Miller Christmas gathering? The idea seemed a good one at the time. Now, she wasn't so sure.

"You're being awfully quiet—worried about this?" he said.

"Stop reading my mind—creeps me out."

"What are you afraid of?"

"Not afraid—I just don't want anybody to misunderstand this."

"And just exactly what is *this*?"

There was a long silence.

"That's the problem—I have no id...I don't want to talk about it. It's going to be fine...forget it... turn here," she said as they pulled onto Rawley Pike.

"Slow down, we're getting close," she said.

He turned into Aunt Belle's driveway as if he'd been there before.

She looked for Jordan and Melinda's van, but it wasn't there.

"Damn, I was hoping Jordan and Melinda would be here so you'd know somebody."

"Relax, Clara Belle, you're bringing a friend to a Christmas party—I'm fine—I'll be myself—you be yourself—easy."

"Maybe for you…it's who these people expect me to be. You watch, the first person we meet will make some comment about a joke."

They got out of the car and walked to the back porch door. Uncle Henry, Hank Jr. and several of the other smokers were over near the wash house. Clara Belle looked longingly as they blew puffs of smoke that circled around their heads. She hadn't had a cigarette since she came home. She inhaled a lung-full of air and blew a stream of breath into the cold winter day. The effect was less than satisfying, even if it looked like the real thing. Mack didn't know about her Tower Room vice.

"Hello, Uncle Henry, Hank Jr.," she said. "Where's Susan?"

"Not coming—hey cuz, got a good one for you…there's this—"

"Later," she said, rolling her eyes at Mack.

"Uncle Henry, Hank Jr., this is my friend, Mack McDonald."

"Nice to meetcha'," said Uncle Henry, sticking out his hand. "Belle says you teach at Dayton High."

"Yes, sir, I teach English and drama."

Clara Belle saw the wheels turning in Hank Jr.'s head and knew what was coming.

"It's cold out here, let's go inside."

As they walked away, she heard Hank Jr., "Weird as ever—hanging out with an old teacher."

"Sorry," she said, "he's always been a royal pain in the ass."

She opened the door. "You ready for this?"

"I was born—"

"No you don't—that's my line."

They walked into the kitchen where Aunt Clara and Aunt Lillian were milling around, looking lost.

"Nothing to do," said Aunt Clara. "No eggs to scramble, no bacon to fry. People just walk in and put stuff on the table."

"Kleine Clara Belle, you are looking peak-ed, yet. They don't feed you good vittles at school?"

"I'm just the same, Aunt Lillian. Mack, these are two of Daddy's sisters, Aunt Clara and Aunt Lillian—this is my friend, Mack McDonald."

They eyed him suspiciously and nodded.

"I get it now," he said. "Clara and Belle—and all this time I thought you'd been named after Howdy Doody's clown."

"Our Clara Belle was tooting her horn long before that one," said Aunt Belle coming in from the dining room. "Right, kid?"

"Aunt Belle, you remember—"

"Sure do, hello again, Mack," and she smiled and patted him on the back.

Once again, Clara Belle suspected conspiracy.

"Help yourself to a Coke here, or—" she nodded toward the side porch.

"Coke is fine," said Mack.

"Me, too," said Clara Belle.

Family began filtering in—cousins Clara Belle hadn't seen for a year, some, more than that. She introduced Mack around—he seemed comfortable—she allowed herself to relax.

The dining room table, where they had played Monopoly long into the night, was filled with assorted foods. Aunt Belle had gotten shrimp and red sauce at the Safeway, there were platters of pimento cheese, egg salad, and chicken salad sandwiches with the crusts cut off. In a chafing dish, Swedish meatballs bubbled above a little Bunsen burner— there were vegetable trays and various chips and dips. The only thing vaguely familiar was Aunt Lillian's plate of sweets. With nothing to prepare or do, everyone stood around awkwardly pretending everything was normal.

Clara Belle motioned to Mack and they walked through the living room to the parlor.

"So this is the famous parlor where your Aunt Belle doled out her wisdom?"

Clara Belle looked around the familiar room.

"Couldn't have survived," she said quietly.

"This the tree she leaves up until Easter?"

"Fake, for the first time—she can leave it up all year now."

There were no presents spilling out from under the tree into the middle of the room—no white envelopes decorating the branches.

Clara Belle shook her head, "Isn't right."

"What?"

"Nothing, come on," she said and led him back through the living room.

Granddaddy Miller had arrived with her parents and was already reclining on the sofa, holding court with returning Millers. Clara Belle decided to wait to introduce Mack.

Melinda and Jordan had arrived, as well as most everyone else. Clara Belle waved across the room. Melinda gave her a thumbs up.

"OK folks, this is the way it's gonna work," said Aunt Belle. "Get a plate at this end, fill it up, get your drink in the kitchen and go anywhere you can find a seat to eat—kids first!"

People served themselves, then wandered through the rooms looking for a place to sit. Plates were balanced awkwardly on laps. Some younger cousins grazed, picking up shrimp and dipping, or munching a sandwich.

"Hey, Clara Belle, Mack," said Melinda, carrying an almost empty plate.

"Hope you didn't bring any of that fire water—I had a bad one the next day," said Mack.

"Pays to be pregnant—I only get morning sickness and it's for a good cause—worth the pain."

"Jordan," said Mack, "good to see you again."

Jordan offered a hand and about half a smile.

"Hello, Mack. Hello, Clara Belle."

Clara Belle picked at her food then went to Granddaddy Miller who had been set up with a TV table and a plate of goodies. She left Mack, who was being grilled by Melinda on the current state of the Civil Rights Movement, and sat down with Granddaddy.

"Well, Granddaddy, what do you think of this?"

"I'm thinking change is not so good for old folks."

"I don't like it either," she whispered.

"Eh?"

She gave him a mouth-raspberry.

"Yah," he said, "no blessing, even."

"Yah," said Clara Belle.

She wandered around making small talk with whomever she met. In every conversation she felt like they were expecting her to do something funny.

She looked across the room where Jordan and her father were deep in conversation with Mack, who looked like he was cornered. She put down her plate and quickly went to them.

"Is this just guy talk, or can I butt in?"

"Talking cars," said her father.

"Cars?" she said, relieved.

"I've been talking to Jordan about that hippie van of his—doesn't really fit in with the academic path he's chosen."

"I made him an offer, but your father underbid and outranked me," said Mack.

"Clara Belle, I've been thinking about your having a car at school next semester," her father said.

Clara Belle was stunned. "I did ask Mom, but—"

"Your mother still needs her Chevy—the VW's safe and would travel well to Greensboro and back—interested?"

"Daddy, that would be great."

"It's a stick shift on the floor," said Jordan. "Can you handle that?"

"I could teach you—it's my fantasy vehicle," said Mack quickly.

"Melinda is going to kill me," said Jordan. "She loves that thing, but I think she'll agree we need a small station wagon for, well…you know."

"We'll work out the details, what you need to get out of it, and getting the title changed in the next few days."

Clara Belle could not believe her good fortune and immediately wondered what the catch was.

With no gift exchange and no other activities, people drifted out and home almost before the empty serving dishes were cleared.

Aunt Belle motioned to Clara Belle—they walked to the parlor.

"Got something for you," said Aunt Belle.

"A present, I hope—this was the pits."

Aunt Belle reached far back under the tree and pulled out a shoebox shaped gift wrapped in Dagwood and Blondie paper.

"I'm giving you this," said Aunt Belle. "Open it when you're ready."

"But…you know I don't—"

"Whenever."

Chapter 12

THE THEATER AND OTHER ACTS

Mack had expected that driving lessons in the van with Clara Belle would be an ideal opportunity for them to be together. The reality of the endeavor turned out to be less than ideal. He had, as a high school English and Drama teacher, developed great patience and solid instruction skills. Apparently, teaching someone you happened to be fond of to drive a stick shift required an entirely different set of attributes. To preserve any headway he had made in this fragile relationship with his former student, he turned the job over to Jordan. Within hours, Clara Belle had mastered the task.

The time with Clara Belle over Christmas had gone better than he had hoped. The awareness of his feelings for her had come upon him gradually. Never, as her teacher, had he once imagined that their spirited conversations were building anything more than a student-teacher bond, which happened quite often with him. Usually he noticed a young girl's crush and immediately kept an appropriate distance. With Clara Belle, this had not been necessary—he had always been comfortable with their lively banter, which had challenged them both. During the past two weeks he had been careful and moved slowly, as Aunt Belle had advised.

Tonight, he was planning what looked suspiciously like a real date.

"So what's the dress code for this event?" asked Clara Belle when he called early in the day.

"For a Coloradoan, I'll be dressed up—button-down, sport coat and kakis."

"The plan?"

"Dinner and the 'theatah.' We're driving to Staunton. A new group there is doing *Our Town*. They've gotten good reviews."

"Reviews—what reviews? We have no drama critics at *The Daily News Record*."

"I just said that to impress you. I have no idea whether it will be crappy local theater or not. If it's really bad, we can make fun of it all the way home."

"Now that sounds like good entertainment—what time?"

"Pick you up at 5:00—they start serving dinner at 6:00."

"OK, see you then," said Clara Belle.

The rest of the afternoon Mack sensed an excitement and anticipation he hadn't felt for a long time. He'd not dated since he came to the area, partly because he hadn't met anyone who interested him and partly because, as a teacher in this very conservative community, he felt he was being watched. He was already suspect, being a twenty-four year old bachelor—he didn't want to be viewed as a playboy. Lord knows, he had never been that.

He looked in the mirror at his attempt at proper date attire and realized he was nervous.

He knocked on Clara Belle's front door. Ben Jr. opened it with an expression that Mack could only describe as "over-fatherly."

"Good evening, Mack—nice to see you again—come on in."

"Thank you, Mr. Miller—good to see you, too."

"Clara Belle will be down in a moment—she and her mother—"

"Hey, Mack," said Clara Belle, coming into the room followed by her mother, who looked over-motherly. But whatever the two of them had done to prepare her for this evening had definitely worked—she looked wonderful.

"Hello, Mack," said Mary Faith.

"Hello, Mrs. Miller—Clara Belle," he said.

There was an awkward silence.

"Let's go," said Clara Belle.

"Not too late," said her mother.

"Good grief, Mom, I'm—"

"I know, I know…just habit."

"The show won't be over until about 11:00 and we'll be coming home from Staunton, so don't expect us before 1:00 or so," said Mack.

He felt like a teenager going to a prom but decided this approach was best for now.

"Don't wait up—and I mean it!" said Clara Belle.

"Drive carefully!"

"Dad! Geez! Let's get out of here," said Clara Belle.

As they walked to the car they passed the VW van.

"How's the driving going?" he asked.

"Got it down—turns out Doo-Dah was the best teacher for me…I mean he knows the car…Oh, hell, let's face it— you just don't have a clue how to teach stick-shift, that's all."

He opened the car door for her. As she crawled in, she said, "I did a real smart thing."

He walked around and got in his side.

"What's that?"

"I offered to pay half of the car."

"Really?"

"Daddy invested my Christmas and birthday money and it did very well over the years. I decided that being a partner in this deal would give me some leverage about how I can or cannot use the merchandise."

"He know your motives?"

"Course not—he just considers it good economics."

Mack planned to stick to familiar subjects—hopefully this would diffuse the uneasiness heavy in the air.

"While you were at school last semester, were you aware of what was going on right in Greensboro?"

"The sit-in at Woolworth's, you mean?"

"That one and all the ones that followed. They staged them in pools, parks, libraries—"

"And my own personal favorite…" Clara Belle said.

"Theaters!" they chorused and laughed.

"I'd sure like to have been there when you pulled that caper."

"You'd have been embarrassed just like everybody else."

"Melinda wasn't," he said.

"She's a mystery to me. I can't figure out how she and Jordan ended up together—so different, those two."

"Opposites attract, I guess," he said.

"Then why do we get along? We're sort of alike."

He didn't have an answer to that one and they both drifted off into their own thoughts. Bringing the conversation back to safer territory he said, "Speaking of theater, how is the drama program at Southampton?"

"Don't know much about it. I haven't seen any of the productions. There's a limit to what they can do at a women's college."

"Ever get the urge to be on stage again?"

"Not really."

"You really have a gift, you know."

"I think I'll stick to academics for a while—have to keep up the grades for my scholarship."

"That means you won't get involved in the sit-ins, either?"

"Probably not—we have reviews and exams when I get back; then I'll be coming home for a long weekend after that. I just don't seem to have that fire I had back at the Virginia Theater—the spark that pushes you to do that kind of thing. Maybe I've lost it for good."

"Sure hope not—it's that fire that makes life worth living."

"Made my life difficult."

"You're older and wiser now," he said.

"And you think that'd make any difference?"

"Worth a try," he said.

~

The show was really bad local theater; the buffet dinner was really bad local food and the nearer they came to home the more obvious it became that they both were thinking about how, exactly, they would handle the end of their first official date. Their vain attempts at conversation and humor were overshadowed by the impending goodbyes, not only for this particular evening, but for Clara Belle's departure for school the next day.

They pulled into the drive and Mack turned off the car. They sat quietly for a few moments. Mack laid his arm casually across the back of the seat. Clara Belle finally scooted across the front seat, looked him straight in the eye and said, "In case you're wondering, I have never been properly kissed. If I go back to school still in that pathetic state, my friend Cravotta will never let me hear the end of it—do I make myself clear?"

"Perfectly," he said.

Chapter 13

THE ROAD-RUNNER RECAP

The freedom she felt as she drove down Route 33 to 29 was exhilarating. She had tuned the radio to a station that played current pop tunes and the volume was cranked to full blast. The music filled every corner of the old van and Clara Belle sang along, in her distinctive alto voice, to the songs she knew and kept rhythm to the ones she didn't.

When she had stopped for gas right outside of Harrisonburg, she bought a pack of Kents. She decided to wait to light up—no need to run into someone she knew. She had also decided not to smoke in the van for obvious reasons—her father had made this kind of trip possible—she was grateful, in spite of herself. Just one of the subtle changes in relationships that had developed this Christmas.

She stopped at a small country store and ordered a cup of coffee and a donut. As she waited, she took out the cigarettes from her purse. She pulled the plastic strip around the side of the pack, flipped the foil on the top and tore off the corner. There was something about that first whiff of tobacco and the look of those fresh little white filters packed tightly together, just waiting to be pulled out, that promised something so satisfying. She turned the pack upside down, tapped the bottom and out slid that first little white cylinder she had denied herself for two weeks. She put the cigarette in her mouth, lit it, took a drag, inhaling deeply and waited for that rush of goodwill to move all through her body. Instead, there quickly followed a coughing fit that wouldn't stop.

"Miss, are you all right?" said the motherly-looking waitress, who set down a cup of coffee and a donut.

"Cough...guess I'm...cough, cough...a little out of... cough...practice."

"You're way too young to smoke," said the waitress.

"You may be...right," she replied, taking a sip of coffee. She put out the cigarette. Maybe she needed to be in the Tower Room playing bridge.

She finished her coffee and donut, paid the bill and continued her trip south.

Alone in the car she began to review the past two weeks in her mind. First and foremost, of course, was Mack. The odd feeling deep in her abdomen that had besieged her ever since last night, which she now recognized had been there before when she thought of him, grabbed her again. How could she explain to anyone, even herself, that the kiss, for which she had waited so many years, was tenderly and perfectly executed by a person who seemed to know exactly what she needed in it. Her whole body tingled with the memory of their goodnight and goodbyes. She smiled when she felt the anticipation of the after-exam return to home when she would see him again. She resisted the urge to light up another cigarette—wasn't that what people did after sex?

The visits with Melinda and Doo-Dah had gone well. Melinda continued to push Clara Belle to reclaim her "Clara Belle-Self" as she called it. She just couldn't seem to let go of her memories of some of Clara Belle's wilder days. They had discussed her discovery of the Episcopal church and Melinda considered this a positive sign. "We Episcopalians can believe most anything and everything without fear of excommunication. Fits you to a 'T.'" Melinda was excited about the baby, but still seemed interested in discovering her own potential and interests. Fart-head, Doo-Dah, had come through for her in teaching her to drive the van. They had laughed and joked and through the laughter came some forgiveness and peace about the years when he had deserted her. He was becoming a little too much like her father, the very proper professor, but as Doo-Dah was becoming more accepting of her, she returned the favor.

Her mother and father remained unchanged. She saw her mother in a new light—saw her giving in to a husband who had aspirations of being a tenured professor and associating with the academic elite of Madison College. Did her mother ever have a life outside their little family? She had given up eighteen years of her life for a strange little girl for whom she had fought battle after battle. Now, what did she have left? Would she ever have the chance to become other than wife and mother? Had she ever even wanted more?

And her rock, Aunt Belle, remained steady, faithful. She looked over at the seat next to her where the Dagwood-and-Blondie, shoe-box-sized box sat like a passenger, still unwrapped.

Her thoughts turned ahead to the next two weeks. There would be reviews for a week, then exams. She wasn't particularly worried about any of her classes. She had always been weak in math but Trig had turned out to be unexpectedly fun. Something about solving those identities was satisfying to her sense of balance and equality, and she had kept an "A" all semester.

She pulled between the two stone pillars at the entrance to school. "Southampton College for Women – 1900." Her spirits, so high for miles, suddenly fell—Cravotta was leaving.

Chapter 14

THE BEGINNING OF THE BEGUINE

Clara Belle pulled up to the back door of her dorm in the van and the first person she saw was Cravotta, looking like she was waiting for the arrival. They hadn't communicated at all during vacation, as if the two worlds they lived in, home and school, were not connected in any way.

"Look at you, Miss hippie-wheels—how'd you manage this?"

"A real sweet deal I couldn't pass up," said Clara Belle.

"What'd you have to GIVE up?" said Cravotta giving her that wide-eyed, scrutinizing look.

"A chunk of my bank account, that's all," she said, then added, "so far. How was your break?"

"Good, I guess. The parents are a little nervous about my plans or lack thereof."

"I thought your folks were wide open to anything you wanted to do—thoroughly hip and cool."

"Within certain bounds. I guess, in the end, all parents want to maintain some semblance of control when they're footing the bills."

She walked around the van.

"Can we take a spin?"

"Let me unload my stuff first—you signed in yet?"

"No, technically, I'm not here yet."

"Good, I'll do the same. We can go get an early dinner before we have to declare ourselves."

Cravotta helped her carry her belongings to Rat Hole. Sandra had not arrived from the north. The little room looked forlorn as if it had missed its occupants. Clara Belle dumped everything on the bed.

"Let's motor," said Clara Belle.

"You seem nauseatingly perky, CB, what's up?"

"Tell you later."

They went back to the van. Just as they were ready to get in, Dr. Norbett's form appeared like a specter from the shadows of one of the brick pillars in the colonnade. She lived in one of the suites in the dorm. She was a stooped, frumpy, maiden-lady with a mysterious past and an even more intriguing present. It was rumored that she entertained, sometimes even in the dorm, various lovers and wrote racy novels under an assumed name. Her prim façade in the classroom belied a much more colorful life. Occasionally, certain pet students were invited to her inner sanctum where the tobacco odor permeated the room cluttered with books, ungraded papers and over-stuffed furniture. Cravotta was one of her pet students.

"Hello, Miss Cravotta, welcome back—excuse me, what was your name again?"

"Miller, Clara Belle Miller."

"Ah, yes, Sacred Clowns, excellent work, Miss Miller."

"Thank you, I—"

"Miss Cravotta, I've been informed that you are giving up your scholarship and leaving us after exams."

"That's right, Dr. Norbett. Southampton is…is…a little confining for my interests. Your class is the only one that doesn't bore me to death."

"Since you're leaving, I'm assuming that you're not attempting to brown-nose me with that remark—however, it has been noted, just the same. Perhaps you and Miss Miller could join me for tea before you fly off into the world at large."

"Just let us know," said Cravotta.

They got into the van and drove to the nearest Big Boy. After they ordered, Cravotta got down to business.

"SOOOOOOO?"

"So what?" said Clara Belle.

"You know damn well what—the Big Mack! Give me all the details."

"Let's just say that I've been properly kissed and leave it at that."

"If I have to—I'll grill you later—what about the rest of your cast of the Clara Belle Show?"

Clara Belle told Cravotta in detail about her encounters with each of the significant family members and noted how relationships had either improved or had stayed about the same.

When she finished, Cravotta leaned back in her chair and said, "Sounds a little too pat for me."

"What the hell's that supposed to mean?"

"Think about it CB—think about it."

~

Clara Belle was back in her room unpacking when she suddenly remembered that she had promised her mother she would call as soon as she got to school—she had also told Mack that she'd call. Sandra hadn't returned; most likely a plane delay.

She walked down the hall to the pay phone and dialed her home number. The phone rang barely once.

"Clara Belle, is that you?" said her mother.

"Hi, Mom, sorry I didn't call before. I went out with a friend to eat dinner and just plain forgot."

"I was beginning to…how was the trip?"

"Good—I got here about 5:00."

"What?...just a minute…Oh, your father wants to know how the van did."

"Tell him it ran like a top… and tell him, thanks again."

There was a pause as she relayed the message.

"Enjoyed having you home—like old times—well, except for Mack, of course...not that we—"

"It was a good visit, Mom. By the way, this is review for exams week and I've got lots of studying to do—don't expect me to call or anything."

"Exams are over when?"

"End of the next week."

"Then you'll be coming home, right?"

"Just for a long weekend—we start second semester the following Tuesday."

"Can't wait."

"OK, then, Mom, bye."

"We love you, Clara Belle, good luck on your exams—I know you'll do well. Goodbye."

"Love you, too."

She hung up the phone and looked to see if anyone else was waiting—the hall was empty. She dialed Mack's number—the phone rang and rang with no answer. She hung up and walked back to her room, wondering why she felt just a little relieved.

Chapter 15

THE SUMMONS TO TEA

Review week was brutal. At Dayton High she had rarely taken notes from a lecture except in Mack's English class—he had insisted on it. Most of the teachers wrote what they wanted students to remember on the blackboard; students copied the material word for word and memorized it word for word. At the beginning of the semester Clara Belle had struggled to learn the skill of sorting out what might be important for tests. There was comparing and contrasting cultures, countries, eras, poets and writers, all at a student's discretion. In other words, she had to learn to think for herself. Once she got the hang of it, she rarely had to ask for anyone's notes. However, the pace had tripled this week and she was, for the first time, apprehensive about whether she could retain the huge amount of material she would be required to master and regurgitate for exams.

"CB, we've been summoned," said Cravotta.

"Summoned for what?" said Clara Belle.

"Dr. Norbett has asked the two of us to high tea in her lair, 4:00 sharp on Saturday—you game?"

"Do we have a choice?"

"You wouldn't want to miss this for the world—besides, it's the last time you'll be able to ride in on my coattails."

"You are such an ego-prick."

"I tell it like it is," said Cravotta.

~

Clara Belle had finally connected with Mack on the phone—she had told him the same thing she told her mother and he understood. However, he had called her several times through the switchboard phone during review week anyway. She wasn't sure how she felt about that—on one hand, there was the pleasant rush she got when the buzz came in her room to go to the hall phone for a conversation with a man like all the other girls. On the other hand, she was annoyed that he didn't respect her wish to be left alone. There was also the constant challenge to put out of her mind the extended time in his car at the end of their date. She blushed when she thought of it, and she thought of it way too much.

With the last of classes and reviews over for the semester and exams looming in two days, tea at Dr. Norbett's was a welcome diversion.

"Is there a dress code for high tea?" she asked Cravotta.

"Have you checked out hostess's fashion sense—early frump—have anything from the '30s?"

"I get the picture—I'll be studying right up to the time we go. I'm having major anxiety over these exams."

"Just study your notes, memorize and organize each and every word—be ready to compare and contrast every event that has ever happened in Western Civilization and every writer in English history as well as give a detailed description of the sexual practices of every culture we've studied in Dr. Norbett's class—she'll love it."

"Just tell me how you know so damn much about this—you're only a freshman, too."

"Wise beyond my years—more importantly, a wise-ass. I fake it."

"Come by my room at 3:45. Anything else I need to know for this meeting?"

"Dare I say, 'just be yourself'?"

Clara Belle raised her middle finger.

~

Dr. Norbett's suite was located in a remote hallway of the underclassman dorm. Cravotta and Clara Belle knocked on the door. There was a shuffling inside, and when it was obvious she was standing on the other side of the door, there was still a long pause.

"Is there a password or something?" whispered Clara Belle.

Dr. Norbett opened the door—a cigarette was dangling from her mouth and the room behind her was thick with smoke. She wore a floor-length red Chinese silk kimono and her frizzy salt and pepper hair framed her puffy face, which had been dabbed with random splotches of lipstick and rouge.

"Miss Cravotta, Miss Miller—how nice of you to come."

"Thank you for inviting us," said Cravotta.

Clara Belle was speechless. The rumors of the disarray in her quarters were greatly underreported. Yes, there was overstuffed furniture, but you couldn't see it for all the rumpled clothes thrown across them. Yes, there were stacks of un-graded term papers, but there were also old newspapers, used paper napkins and tissues scattered on the floor and every table in the room. However, in the large bay window looking out on the courtyard was a small table with three chairs surrounding it. In this little oasis, there was no clutter of any kind. The table was neatly laid with a delicate china tea set on an embroidered lace cloth. In the center of the table was a crystal vase with a single pink rosebud that perfectly matched the flower pattern in the china set.

"Please have a seat, ladies," she said, as she stubbed out her cigarette in one of the many ashtrays scattered throughout the room.

Cravotta and Clara Belle sat down. Dr. Norbett seated herself and began to pour the steaming tea into the china cups in front of each of them.

"This is a ginger tea I found in a village in Guam—quite delicate. I find it needs neither sugar, milk nor lemon, but I have them all if you wish."

They each sipped their tea in silence and followed their hostess's advice.

"Miss Miller, your interest in other cultures, where did this develop?"

"To be honest, in your class—I'd never even heard of Margaret Mead. I went to a small country high school in Virginia. Virginians think they are the only culture."

Dr. Norbett chuckled, "I understand—I'm from Massachusetts—they think the same thing."

"Your collaboration on sacred clowns was outstanding. I particularly enjoyed learning about the Native Eskimo tribe in Canada. I'd never come across that particular culture. Where did you get your information?"

"Some Canadian woman wrote a book based on interviews with the women there who passed down the traditions orally," explained Clara Belle. "After the missionaries completely fuc... pardon, destroyed their traditions they went underground. The clowns were always women and were—"

"I read the paper, Miss Miller," said Dr. Norbett.

"Sorry, I get a little overly excited about things sometimes."

"One might call that passion."

"Dr. Norbett, have you thought about what I mentioned?" said Cravotta.

"Indeed, I have. That's why I invited you both here."

Dr. Norbett and Cravotta looked at each other conspiratorially. Clara Belle looked from one to the other.

"Why don't you tell her?" said Dr. Norbett.

"I was given a full scholarship to major in anthropology. I'm leaving—I've asked Dr. Norbett to recommend that it be given to you."

"But I already have a full scholarship," said Clara Belle.

"Yours, from what you've said, is a general one, for no particular major, am I right?"

"Yours different?"

"Mine requires a major in anthropology and here's the good part—it will pay for field work anywhere in the world you want to go after your junior year."

"Wow," was all Clara Belle could say.

"Miss Miller, are you at all interested?"

"I'd need some time to think about it—I haven't even considered what my major might be. I like anthropology, I do but—"

"You don't have to make a decision now—I just need to know during the next month to begin the process of getting it in place for your sophomore year."

"Seems like a huge decision in a short time to me," said Clara Belle.

"Don't think so much, CB. Follow your gut, follow your gut."

Chapter 16

THE THEORY IN REAL TIME

Exam week was one of those periods when Clara Belle wasn't sure at which speed she wanted time to go. She would be greatly relieved when her exams were over, but she didn't want the time between them to go so quickly that she wouldn't be prepared for each one. She was savoring every last moment with Cravotta, but anticipating her return trip to Virginia. She couldn't wait to see what would happen with Mack when they met again—she was a wreck with feelings of uneasiness.

"CRAVOTTA! I've got a theory," she said the day before exams began.

"Something you dreamed up on one of your walks, I assume."

"Well, you won't talk to me about this stuff," said Clara Belle.

"So what is it now, you have a holy vision?"

"You are such a shit," said Clara Belle.

"And that, my friend, you are going to miss most of all."

"I have a theory about time—I'm going to experiment with something eastern religions do," said Clara Belle.

"You're going to shave your head and meditate?"

"I'm going to practice the presence of the 'now.' "

"The who?"

"No, 'now.' "

"You and Einstein—enlighten me."

"You know how sometimes you can't wait until something happens in the future and it seems to take forever to get there?"

"Like the time I have left here?"

"Right, and other times, when you are really enjoying something, the time just flies by and you want to hold it back."

"Like when you're locking lips with the Mack-ster."

"CRAVOTTA! Be serious. Here's my theory. What if you were completely in the moment with whatever you were doing, not thinking about what might happen next or what happened just before, and time would go at just the speed it was meant to and you wouldn't be anxious or frustrated. What do you think?"

Cravotta pondered the possibilities.

"Worth a try—so let's enjoy this moment because I'm going—"

"No, no, no—see there, you've already moved out of the moment. NOW, CRAVOTTA! NOW!"

For the next five days she did her best to test her theory—to be totally in the present. It wasn't easy and slowly there came an awareness of how little of her life she had lived this way. She caught herself constantly going back and forth in any given moment.

Easiest were the exams themselves. She sat in that classroom with her bluebook and #2 pencil, her brain filled to the brim with information she had stored there, and let it spill out effortlessly in the moment. The experience was exhilarating. When she left each exam, she vowed to not think about how she had done but moved immediately into the moments of studying for the next exam and so on through the week. The result was a time with little worry, little anxiety.

Other parts of life were not so simple in the moment. She and Cravotta couldn't help talking about what Cravotta would be doing after she left school and how they would miss their friendship. Dr. Norbett wanted a decision about the scholarship. Her mother constantly called and talked about how she just couldn't wait until Clara Belle came home and Mack was pushing her to find out about when there would be a sit-in—he wanted to come to Greensboro next semester. The "NOW" was hard.

Thursday afternoon after her last exam, Clara Belle went to Cravotta's room where she had finished packing. Boxes and suitcases were piled neatly by the door, ready to be picked up by her parents tomorrow morning.

"Hey, CRAVOTTA!" said Clara Belle, "let's put on our woolies and go and just 'BE!'"

The two of them walked silently down the path toward the lake, which had a skim of ice from the below freezing temperature of the past week. The campus was still, quiet before the noise of the exodus of students after exams.

They sat down on the concrete benches at the edge of the lake. Clara Belle had brought along a small transistor radio, which she tuned to the classical station. They blew clouds of winter breath as they listened to Vivaldi's "Four Seasons—Winter Movement."

Suddenly, there was a single snowflake, then another, then thousands, millions of white dancing lace in the air, landing on the frozen lake. Without a word, Clara Belle and Cravotta rose simultaneously from the bench, and began twirling to the music, arms out-stretched, tongues out-stuck, catching the snowflakes. Around and around they spun like two little girls, laughing and laughing with tears rolling down their cheeks.

"NOW," they said together, "NOW!"

Chapter 17

THE RIDDLE OF LIFE

Clara Belle and Cravotta leaned up against the packed VW van, as if it could bear some of the weight they were feeling— having no idea how to manage this goodbye.

The night before they had gone to the Tower Room and stayed up smoking and talking until early this morning. There was a sense of finality to this goodbye and no theory of living in the now could soften the pain of that awareness.

They were both silent.

Clara Belle finally broke the silence, "CRAVOTTA! I have a question that I need you to answer before you...before we...I need to know something."

"What's that, CB?" said Cravotta.

"That night during Rat Week, in the dorm, when those two girls—"

"Ancient history—don't want to talk about it."

"I don't need to know what they did, that's not important—I could see you were OK the next morning. What's important for me to know is...I don't get... why did you go with them? You could have gotten out of it, yelled bloody murder or something. You didn't have to go—why did you? I need to know why."

Cravotta waited a beat and then smiled a sly, Cravotta-esque smile.

"You must swear on the Mackster's sweet bootie that you will never tell this to another living soul—I mean no one—understand?"

"I swear," said Clara Belle, raising her right hand in the air.

"I knew I had pushed the bimbo too far that day on the Rat-green and I knew full well I'd have to pay for it sooner or later. It was only a matter of time until Billingham and Company would create a plan to fully humiliate me and let me know who was in charge. They'd also do it in a way that I'd not want to tell anyone—and I haven't.

"That night when they came to my room, I was sound asleep—I didn't even hear them come in the door. Before I was fully awake, they had already put a blindfold over my eyes and stuffed a rag in my mouth. Sure, I knew I could make a ruckus and my roommate would wake up, but I had already decided that when this went down, which I knew it would, I would go along."

"But why would you do that? I don't understand."

"Nothing they could do to me could touch me unless I let it—they knew they couldn't hurt me physically or they'd be in trouble for sure, so they tried to humiliate me psychologically. They took me to one of the rooms where two other lovely ladies were waiting. I won't go into the specifics, but they kept me up until 4:00 in the morning, stark naked and said things to me that no proper Southampton Lady should even know about. When I finally went back to my room, I knew I had won. They didn't know that, but I did—what mattered was, if they believed they had won, it was over and I was free."

"So you chose what happened—isn't that a little masochistic?" said Clara Belle.

"I didn't choose what happened—I only chose my response and I'm stronger for it."

"But if they thought they won, didn't they? Don't you care that they don't know how you see it?"

"That's the trouble with you southern women, always worrying about what someone else is thinking—that's your barometer for what you think, who you are. I don't give a rat's ass what they took away from that night—I only care about what I learned about myself. It'll catch up with them one day."

"Karma rules, right?" said Clara Belle.

"Now you're talking."

"My Aunt Belle told me once that she was the only one who stood up to her stepmother. The other kids would run away and Aunt Belle would just stand there, black eyes flashing, hands on her hips, defying Grandmother Miller. She paid the price, but, in the end, I guess she won, too. That's probably why she's the rock she's been for me all these years—she always knew who she was and stood up for herself. So, now comes the hard question I have to ask myself."

"What's that, CB?"

"I saw them take you that night—I was hiding in the bathroom in Rat Hole. Why the hell didn't I do something?"

Cravotta's eyes widened with surprise and then quickly softened.

"The same question half the world asked after World War Two, 'Why didn't we do something?' "

"What's the answer, CRAVOTTA!? You would have done something if it had been me."

"I'm not so sure of that. I might have done exactly the same thing—we're all chicken-shits at one time or another—key is being conscious of our cowardice. If we're fortunate, maybe we learn something, we forgive ourselves and try not to do it the next time."

"Can you forgive me?" said Clara Belle.

"Forgive yourself—I'm fine. Now, for god's sake, let's change this morbid subject and say a proper goodbye."

Clara Belle coughed—Cravotta blew her nose.

They stood there, not knowing what to do next.

Clara Belle was the first to speak.

"What's invisible and smells like carrots?" she said glumly.

"You're shitting me, right? Is this any time for a riddle?"

"Perfect timing—we both need a little giggle and this one is more like a Zen koan—once again, what's invisible and smells like carrots?"

"I don't know, Clara Belle," said Cravotta. "What's invisible and smells like carrots?"

Clara Belle pulled herself away from the van, stretched herself to her full height of five feet. "Bunny Farts—Ta-Dah!" she said and raised her arms in the air.

"CB, you are one for the ages—how far did you go back for that one?"

"The beginning, Cravotta—to the very beginning!"

~

Clara Belle drove north on Route 29. She was beginning to get thirsty and needed a cigarette and gas. As she neared Danville, she saw a sign "Exxon Ahead - Juncture of 29N/S - 58E/W."

She continued on a few miles and saw the station. "Gas—30 cents a gallon," said the sign out front.

"What a rip-off," she said pulling up to the pump.

She filled the tank, pulled up to the little store and went inside for a Pepsi and to pay for the gas. Outside she saw a picnic table under an old elm tree over to the side—she sat down and lit up a cigarette. It tasted stale and awful—too many the night before in the Tower Room—maybe she'd quit—maybe not.

She stubbed out the cigarette and walked back to the van. She patted the side affectionately. "My freedom wagon," she said.

She got in the van, closed the door and looked once again at the unwrapped tin box on the front seat.

"Oh, what the hell," she said as she tore at Blondie and Dagwood. She unlatched the lid and opened the familiar box. Out fluttered a piece of paper. On it, written in Aunt Belle's scrawl were the words, "It was you who created my inmost self, and put me together in my mother's womb; for all these mysteries I thank you: for the wonder of myself—Psalm 139."

She sat there for quite awhile, holding the note in her hand. Then she carefully placed it back in the tin box, closed the lid and put the box on the floor behind her.

She started the van and began pulling out of the filling station. She looked at the sign in the road ahead—Route 29/North/South, Route 58/East/West. She searched her memory for a suitable quote from her extensive reading of the past semester. The first and most obvious one was from Robert Frost—"Two paths diverged in the wood—" she quickly dismissed it and chose another.

She looked at her image in the rearview mirror and said aloud to herself, "As the great sage Yogi Berra says, 'When you come to a fork in the road—take it.' "

AND SHE DID!

THE BEGINNING

"In the cracks between many rituals and prayers, the Cosmic Giggle emerges and overtakes even the most solemn, the most holy."

Rachel Naomi Remen
"My Grandfather's Blessings"

Afterword

Becoming Clara Belle is a work of fiction. After reading the manuscript, someone who knows literary genre suggested that, more precisely, it is a fictional memoir. I believe that category describes this story as well as any.

With two exceptions, all of my characters are composites or completely fictional. Clara Belle is autobiographical in one sense but she also embodies the many children with whom I have worked throughout my career—those with extraordinary limitations and differences as well as extraordinary gifts.

The Miller family is based on my own family of origin, who have for six generations lived on a farm in Rockingham County, Virginia. Clara Belle's parents, aunts, uncles and cousins as well as Jordan and Melinda are fictional but familiar.

Dayton High School emerges as a character in herself and I hope that I have done her justice. I was educated in this wonderful place from first grade until my junior year in high school when a new consolidated school was built. Those years, the teachers like Miss Heatwole, and the friends I made there are dear to me and shaped me in more ways than I can express.

Aunt Belle is one of the exceptions I mentioned. The character is the literary embodiment of the aunt after whom I was named. The situations and stories surrounding her are fictional but I in no way exaggerated her essence, her generous spirit nor her profound influence in my life.

Carley Simon has a song "You're so Vain, You Prob'ly Think this Song is About You" that comes to mind when I try to explain the fictional character, Mack. Which one, of all the interesting and influential male teachers and professors I have encountered through the years, would not want to be the inspiration for Mack, Clara Belle's perfect muse? I'll keep that one to myself.

Southampton College is a fictional school based on my own alma mater in Richmond, Virginia. My fellow classmates will recognize Dr. Norbett, as well as other familiar milestones of our freshman year there. The fact that I completely skipped Clara Belle's college years in every other version before this one is significant.

As for CRAVOTTA!, she's as real as my memory has allowed. I'm still searching for her, without success, on the Web. I changed her first name but found it impossible to alter, in any way, the visceral impact and the memory that surname evokes. She left after our freshman year. The fact is, I didn't know her well at all, but something about her strong personality stayed with me. I invented her family, and none of what CRAVOTTA says or does in this story ever happened. I hadn't thought of her for almost fifty years, when one day, as I was writing Clara Belle into college, she mysteriously appeared on the page. Her presence and the awareness she revealed through her relationship with Clara Belle have, in no small part, altered what I know concerning who I am and who I want to be.

Wherever you are, CRAVOTTA! I hope you won't mind.

No one was more surprised than I was when Clara Belle came to the crossroads in that VW Van and the book ended there. In every version before I had continued for years and years ad nauseam.

I knew this was where I had to leave her. I ask you, the reader, to consider which way she might choose to go and why you personally wish her to take that path. Perhaps you will discover something about your own journey and the choices you have already made or have yet to make.

Acknowledgments

When a book takes twelve years to complete, there are many people to thank, for many reasons.

To my genetic family of origin, all the way back to 1500 AD Switzerland, I am eternally grateful for the strand of DNA that gave me the love of story-telling, bank barns and snowstorms. I am indebted to my immediate family of origin, for an upbringing that, I now realize, was unique and precious in this out-of-kilter world. I thank my parents, siblings, aunts, uncles, cousins, grandparents and Sunny Slope Farm. "The boundary lines have fallen for me in pleasant places; behold, I have a goodly heritage." Psalm 16:6

There have been many special children with whom I have worked and played through the years. There were those with huge challenges and those who were merely "different" in some way; each one challenged and inspired me. I also salute the parents who served as untiring advocates in a medical and educational environment that often ignored the potential of these children.

I thank Jane Bowden and Peggy Fosse for interviews concerning growing up during the 1940s and 1950s with a sibling who has mental challenges. Most children of that day were sent off to institutions, while these particular families chose to keep their own at home. Their insights helped me depict the complex emotions that Jordan felt for Clara Belle—the devotion and protection, the embarrassment and guilt.

I am grateful to my dear friend, Debbie Johnson, who I met 25 years ago serving on a Very Special Arts Committee here in Lynchburg. Debbie was born with Cerebral Palsy. In spite of her significant physical challenges, she graduated from college, earned a Master's degree and has served in this community on many boards and committees that address the needs of people with disabilities. Her friendship and her life have shown me that we are only limited by our reluctance to see the possibilities. Debbie is extremely intelligent and outrageously funny. She is a Christian in the best sense, whose faith is solid as a rock, but doesn't mind an off-color joke once in awhile. There is a lot of Debbie in Clara Belle and a lot of Clara Belle in Debbie.

Sarah Raessler, thank you for one of Clara Belle's best lines, "I was born to love and I was born to be funny." Thanks to Deborah, her mother, for other insights into the life of a family in today's world who has a child with Down's Syndrome.

Early on, I imposed on friends to read my attempts at telling Clara Belle's story. Sue Currie, Patricia Kirtley, Betsy Garrard, Patty Worsham, Cheryl Hailey and Betty Martin all gave me encouragement to continue and believed that her story needed to be told. My voice teacher, Florence Vickland Calder, was in a nursing home nearing her death when I read some of Clara Belle's adventures aloud to her. This elegant lady, for years a primo soprano in New York, retired here in Lynchburg, Virginia. She surprised and delighted me when she divulged that Clara Belle reminded her of herself as a child. Anyone who knew "Vickie" might be a little surprised at that admission!

Along the way, I made an attempt to "Become Clara Belle" in the literal sense. I had given up on writing the book and decided to dress up like Clara Belle and tell stories and sing songs with the children at my church during an Epiphany Season Program. I thank my friend, Mary Fontaine Harris, who was a collaborator in this experiment. The "Clara Belle the Clown Show" was a flop—Clara Belle "on the Road" was a very short trip. Since there were no further bookings, the costume went to the attic with my box of manuscripts, the tent folded, and Clara Belle once again went into hiding. Fontaine encouraged me and took some wonderful photos to document this phase of the Clara Belle saga. From this experience, I learned that "being Clara Belle" was hard.

Finally, to the Reverend Suzanne Currie, Mary Strate Bahm, EdD, Licensed Clinical Psychologist, Betsy Garrard, an utmost-worthy English teacher, Glenn Buck, EdD, Professor of Special Education, Lynchburg College, and Linda Buck, Special Education teacher, my thanks for going above and beyond writing the blurbs for the cover. Even though I emphatically stated that what they were about to read was the final version ("it is what it is"), each had the courage to ignore that statement and offer crucial suggestions that ultimately served to make a much improved book.

Before I launched into this final attempt at writing Clara Belle's story, I knew that there was something I wanted to do. My pastor, The Reverend Diane Vie, lovingly agreed to let me place the large box, overflowing with materials from the past eleven years, on the altar at church. She placed her hands on that box and prayed a special blessing. I knelt at the altar and she did the same for me.

God's guidance in this journey, Clara Belle's and mine, has been abundant. Above all, I am thankful for that.

About the Author

Libby Layne was born in Rockingham County, Virginia. Since graduating from Westhampton College, University of Richmond, with a BS in Music Education, she has shared her love for music with children in schools, choirs, at churches and in the communities where she has lived. After earning an MEd in Counseling at Lynchburg College, her interest in the therapeutic use of music and sound led her to work with children with a variety of disabilities: Down's Syndrome, ADD, Pervasive Development Disorder, emotionally disturbed children and teenagers, children with learning difficulties, mental retardation and autism.

In 1997 she chronicled her study of the vocal communications of Atlantic Spotted Dolphins and their effects on four individuals with autism in her book, *The Sound of the Dolphin's Psalm*.

She currently lives with her husband of 48 years in Lynchburg, Virginia.

This is her first novel.